Christmas, *Actually*

A Holiday Collection

velvet morning
press

ISBN-13: 978-0692467626
ISBN-10: 0692467629

Cover design by Ellen Meyer and Vicki Lesage

Note from the Editors

The holiday season, from Thanksgiving through the New Year, has so many facets, offers so many ways to celebrate—or not celebrate—that it almost begs us to express all of this through words. Who doesn't have a funny holiday story? Who hasn't rejoiced or mourned during this season, which comes as a blessing for some and a torment for others?

This time of year, good or bad, is linked to storytelling and memories. From childhood tales of Santa Claus to true stories that have touched us, inspiration is never very far. What better starting point for an author?

In this collection, six authors write stories of romance, tragedy, hope and laughter. We see the holidays through drama, through humor, through the emotions that have touched most of us one holiday season or another.

Whether you are celebrating Christmas, Hanukkah or Kwanzaa, whether you love big New Year's celebrations or prefer staying home with a good book, we hope you find the holiday spirit in *Christmas, Actually* and make it a part of your season.

Vicki Lesage and Adria J. Cimino
Velvet Morning Press

P.S. To kick off the collection, Vicki Lesage shares a traumatizing yet humorous Christmas tale. Happy Holidays!

Table of Contents

Christmas Past

"No space of regret can make amends for one life's opportunity misused."
— Charles Dickens, *A Christmas Carol*

All I Want For Christmas Is My Two Front Teeth

Vicki Lesage

I'm mildly obsessed with teeth. That's what happens when you have not one but two traumatic dental experiences.

When I was a kid, I fell off a row of bleachers and knocked out my two front teeth.

I totally deserved it.

My mom and I picked up my younger brother, Stephen, from basketball practice, and I tormented him as usual. I chased him up the bleachers, then shouted, "First one down wins! Last one's a loser!"

As it was the middle of winter, I was wearing my snazzy high-heeled snow boots. I was eleven. I had no business wearing high-heeled snow boots. I also had no business running up and down bleachers in said snow boots.

Knowing I would never defeat my speedy brother by running down the bleachers, I opted to jump off the side instead. One of my heels got caught on the edge, and I face-planted on the basketball court. It hurt so bad it almost didn't hurt at all.

Blood splattered everywhere. Girls screamed, and guys said stuff like "Dude, is that Steve's sister?" and "Some girl broke her face."

Hey, that's MY face you're talking about!

My mom rushed over, helped me up, and escorted me to the bathroom.

The moment of truth: looking in the mirror. I thought maybe I'd broken my nose or busted my lip. But no, one of my front teeth was loose, and a huge piece of the other one had chipped off.

An image came to my head, of future me in a wood-paneled boardroom trying to convince a CEO to agree to my marketing plan. My papers were prepared, and I was dressed in a sharp suit. But the CEO just kept staring at my chipped tooth and wouldn't take me seriously.

That was it. My life was over. My career had ended before I'd even made it out of childhood.

Our family dentist, Dr. Sheinbein, fixed my smile a few days later. He did a decent job, and his repairs lasted for years, even though upon close inspection (which I did way more than necessary) you could see my teeth weren't perfect.

In my late twenties, I decided to have them redone. X-rays showed that each tooth needed a root canal, and I could get pearly white crowns at the same time. And why not throw in a little professional teeth whitening?

I'd booked an appointment with the cosmetic dentist Dr. Sheinbein had recommended and would be seeing him on my upcoming trip to the U.S. Much as I enjoyed Paris, I was looking forward to going home for the holidays, not just to fix my teeth and to see my family, but for a change of scenery since I'd recently broken up with my long-time French-Brazilian boyfriend, Pierre. While the break-up hadn't been traumatic, it still represented a huge change in my life.

"Hello, Vicki! Come right this way, and we'll get started." The dentist I'd be spending the next five hours with was friendly and welcoming. He whitened and molded and photographed. Then we were ready for the masterpiece to begin.

"Here's an iPod to help pass the time," his equally friendly assistant said.

I managed to kill half an hour just figuring out how the damn thing worked. As a math nerd, I know how to program computers, and I enjoy differential equations more than one should, but am clueless when it comes to these newfangled gadgets.

Once I finally got it to play, I tuned out as drills buzzed and whirred. I even fell asleep for a while.

When I woke up, I noticed the iPod had stopped. I'd been in the dentist's chair so long it had run out of batteries! Considering the cost of the dental work, I figured it was acceptable to ask for a recharge or another iPod. Who knew how much longer I'd be stuck there? Musical distraction was just what I needed.

"Ekthuse me, but thith ith out of batterieth," I spit out. Um, why did I sound like Daffy Duck? I don't know what I thought root canals and crowns were before I started the appointment, but feeling two metal spikes with my tongue, I suddenly realized I no longer had two front teeth. The teeth I'd known for more than two decades were gone, replaced by vampire fangs.

The dentist must have seen the expression of terror on my face, as he quickly reassured me, "Almost finished! All we have to do is slide the teeth on, and you'll be on your way!"

So I guess they'd forgotten about the iPod. I had to endure the rest of the appointment acutely aware of the work being done in my mouth. I was fearful of the results.

"All done," he said, after what seemed like centuries,

raising the chair to a seated position. "Let's have a look!"

He handed me a mirror, then stepped back, beaming with pride.

I hesitantly opened my mouth and smiled at my reflection.

Oh. My. God.

I'd thought nothing could be worse than my metal Dracula fangs, but I'd been wrong. In their place were the fakest teeth I'd ever seen. First, they were slightly yellower than the rest of my teeth. Didn't we bleach my teeth for a reason? So that the crowns would be the same shade of sparkling white?

Second, they were huge. Way bigger than my old teeth. They practically needed their own zip code. I was one step away from Bugs Bunny.

But most importantly, my "teeth" were actually ONE BIG TOOTH WITH A LINE SCRATCHED DOWN THE MIDDLE to make it look like two teeth.

I'm not kidding.

I started to hyperventilate. I couldn't believe I'd been tortured for five hours to end up looking like a cartoon character.

"What do you think?" the dentist asked, oblivious to my concern. "They look great, huh?"

"Um, I have to go," I said, handing him the mirror, grabbing my purse and coat, and running the heck out of there.

I stopped by the front desk to pay, even though it seemed a crime to be charged for this.

"Hi honey," the smiling receptionist said. "Ooh, your teeth are beautiful! Your total is $4,567. Will you be paying by check or credit card?"

"Credit card," I squeaked. I was about to have a breakdown. Between the astronomical cost and the Bugs Bunny tooth (singular), I was on the verge of tears. Oh, please no, don't let me cry in the waiting room! But as soon as I thought about crying, the waterworks started up.

"Oh honey, what's the matter?" the receptionist asked, processing my credit card as slowly as humanly possible.

I had to get out of there. Why was this taking so long? And could I please stop crying?

In between sniffles I managed to reply. "I'm so upset with my tooth. It's ONE tooth, and it's big and yellow and ugly. And expensive. And I wanted to look good now that I'm single because my boyfriend and I broke up!" I was wailing at that point.

Mercifully, she finished with my credit card and handed it back to me. "Well, if it makes you feel any better, my husband just died."

What? How would that make me feel better? Now instead of wallowing in misery over my first-world problem and expensive rabbit tooth, I had to come up with something sympathetic to say to this grieving widow.

"I'm really sorry to hear that. That must be tough," I mumbled. "I'm sorry, but I have to go." I grabbed my stuff and ran out the door, only then noticing the two other people in the waiting room. As if the ordeal hadn't been embarrassing enough, now there were witnesses!

In the end, it all worked out. What the dentist had failed to tell me was that this tooth (I refuse to call it "teeth") was only temporary until my crowns came in. That's what all the molds and photos were about. I had to sport my Bugs Bunny tooth for the longest two weeks of my life, but eventually, I was the proud owner of two shiny, white, perfectly shaped teeth.

Just in time for Christmas.

Nice Wheels

Katie Rose Guest Pryal

Six Weeks Until Christmas

Barbara woke to a dark sense of wrongness. She opened her eyes to the stark white of her ceiling, the bright orange of her comforter. They were the same as every morning. Unchanged. And then, that breathless bolt of pain, *Bob*, lanced through her like it did every morning, every morning since he'd died.

She sat up quickly, squeezing the comforter between her fingers until they hurt.

She considered whether to cry. She was so accustomed to the pain of grief at this point that she had the choice. She could cry now, in her orange bed. Or, she could cry later, unexpectedly, when she would think she saw the back of his head in the hospital corridor, or when she would see a car like his baby blue Acura—the same color as his eyes—zipping through traffic.

Cry now, in private? Or cry later, during rounds, in front of the other residents?

The tears came.

❦

Twenty minutes after she awoke, she climbed into her Tesla and drove to the medical center. After Bob, her husband, was killed—his plane shot down by enemy fire in the borderlands of Pakistan and Afghanistan—she received money for her medical school tuition. She used the rest to buy the first decadent thing she'd ever owned, the red Model-S she now navigated into the parking deck across from the hospital where she worked as a medical resident in dermatology.

It was the second Wednesday in November, and even though she was attending school in North Carolina where it was supposed to be warm, and even though she was from Boston where it was often below freezing, the chill bit through to her bones. She pulled her large down coat close around her body, hugging herself, and trotted across the sky bridge that connected the parking deck to the hospital. The morning wind cut through even her coat's thick pockets of quilted down.

Will I ever feel warm again?

❦

She skipped through the sliding glass doors and ran to catch an elevator door that was about to close. At the last moment, a hand reached out to open it for her. She stepped on, glancing at the man who'd held the door. He wore the same pale-blue scrubs as she, marking him as another resident. She'd seen him before, in the cafeteria, in the coffee shop in the lobby. It wasn't hard to learn everyone's faces.

But Barbara made no effort to get to know anyone here. She'd come to North Carolina to get away from Boston, from Bob's family and from her own. She needed a new land to start a new life. She needed to be away from eyes that would judge how she mourned, how much and when. So when Bob died during her last year of medical school, she filled out a slew of new residency applications, flinging confetti at a United States map, not caring where she landed so long as it was far away from anyone she'd known before. From anyone who'd known her and Bob together.

"Good morning," the resident said to her.

She nodded, not meeting his eyes, not even turning to look at him.

"It's freezing out," he said.

She nodded again.

"Too early to be up in this cold."

This time she looked at him, annoyed, her practiced glare telling him, *Get the point, buddy. I do not want to talk to you about the weather.*

His appearance startled her, though. He looked down at her—*damn he was tall*—and he was grinning. Like he *knew* he was annoying her, and he kept doing it anyway.

The elevator doors opened.

"See you around," he said, stepping off.

Chris had to stop himself from whistling as he made his way down the corridor to the other sports medicine fellows gathering at the counter at the end of the hall. He couldn't believe his luck, catching Barbara in the elevator like that. He'd been trying to get her alone for weeks.

Everyone in the hospital said she was as cold as a stone. Really, they said a lot nastier things than that, especially the sports medicine fellows. Then again, sports docs were essentially overgrown twelve-year-olds, so you shouldn't be surprised by anything they said, especially about girls.

You'll never crack that one, Dominic had told him. *She's the ice princess*, another had warned him. *She's got nice wheels, though*, Jericho had said.

Chris agreed. He'd seen her jogging around campus one evening, and she had stellar legs.

But Chris didn't think Barbara was a stone or made of ice. He just thought she had some secrets. Chris would know. He had some secrets of his own. When Jericho had complained about having to replace one of the Pirellis on his Merc, Chris had laughed and played along, jabbing him about his sob story.

Chris drove a 1972 Ford Ranger pick-up truck that didn't have any heat. And he couldn't afford to fix it even though this winter was one of the coldest on record.

When he'd told Barbara it was too early and too cold to be heading in to work? He'd meant it. He still couldn't feel his fingers.

He let the other guys think he drove the truck to be—What did they call it? *Retro*. Sure. His bank account was so retro it never had more than double-digits in it.

Because Chris definitely had secrets. But he'd never tell Jericho or the other guys. They wouldn't even know how to process what it meant to be poor, so poor that he used his bleak fellow's salary to support his mom and sisters back home in Texas.

But Chris could keep up an act. No problem. He'd done it for years.

"What's up, Snake!" Jericho called out to Chris, using his basketball nickname.

"Who's got the coffee?" Chris asked.

"Domino."

Chris turned to Dominic, who handed him his large black coffee. "Thanks man." The heat of the coffee cup seeped into Chris' frozen fingers, and he had to stop himself from sighing out loud.

"Stop thanking me," Dominic said, annoyed. "It isn't

a gift."

"Just being polite." Chris smiled, rubbing in his position of superiority a little longer. Next week, he might be the one buying the coffees.

But he doubted it.

Every Sunday, the sports fellows played a basketball game, one with a wager. The losing team had to buy the winning team coffee every morning the following week. Chris' team had only lost once all year. Chris had a bit of an unfair advantage, having played small forward at a Big Ten basketball program on scholarship.

He considered the weekly coffees a rich-boy tax. It wasn't much, but perhaps just enough to make up for the lack of heat in his truck. Coffees ran three bucks in the coffee shop downstairs. He wouldn't be able to afford that anyway.

Morgan walked up while Chris was enjoying his first sip. Morgan was Chris' only real friend in the program. Maybe that was because Morgan was the only black person in the program, another odd man out like Chris. For whatever reason, they connected. He was also the only person Chris had ever talked to seriously about Barbara—because Morgan would speak respectfully of her, and he wouldn't blab to the other guys about how Chris felt.

Morgan grabbed his coffee from Dominic, and then the four of them—Jericho, Dom, Chris and Morgan—joined the larger group of fellows for rounds.

"I hear one of the lady soccer stars came in with a knee injury," Jericho said. "A tall, blonde booter-with-hooters."

Most of the other guys whistled and laughed, rubbing their hands together.

Jesus help me, Chris thought. *I will never make it till the end of the year.*

‰

Later that day, Barbara sat on a stool in a small surgical suite, removing a pre-cancerous mole from a woman's neck. The work required precision—no, perfection. And perfect concentration. That's one reason she'd picked dermatology as her specialty.

A surgical residency, too, would have required precision and concentration. But surgery wasn't for her. She knew that now that she was nearing the end of her second year of her derm residency. She'd deliberately picked a field that only required her to pay attention to the surfaces of things. One that didn't require her to look too deeply.

Dig too deeply, sometimes, and you find rotten things. Better to work with what you can see.

She laced delicate stitches along the woman's skin, knotted off the last one, then set her instruments on the tray. Her medical assistant would finish covering the wound and clean the suite.

"It will heal nicely," she told the woman. "You won't even have a scar."

"That's incredible," she said. "How do you do that?"

Barbara wiggled her gloved fingers. "Magic hands." They laughed together. It felt good to laugh.

Once in the hall, Barbara checked her watch. It was time for her weekly call to Arthur.

‰

She entered the small break room the residents shared. She sat on the cot, leaning back against the cool white wall, and opened her laptop. She put on her headphones and logged into the secure tel-com application approved by the military division Arthur worked for. Then she waited. Sometimes she had to wait a while for him to join her online. Sometimes he never made it at all. She worried about him, but not like she'd worried about Bob.

That's how she knew she didn't love Arthur.

She sat on the cot waiting for him, staring at the black screen. Finally, a flicker, and then his face.

"Hey babe," Arthur said, smiling his handsome half-smile, reaching his finger to touch the screen.

"Hey," she said. "What've you been up to?"

"This and that."

They started every conversation this way. Barbara knew he couldn't tell her what he did. But it made him happy she asked. So she always asked. She wanted to make Arthur happy.

"You still good at flying?" she asked.

"Still the best," he said. "Still coming home to you."

Barbara glanced away from the screen. She counted quickly—Arthur had eight more weeks before his return, just after New Year's.

"Arthur, I—"

"Don't say anything, babe," he said. "Just." A pause, while he rubbed his hand over his mouth. "Just let me think about it while I'm here these last few weeks. And then we'll work out the details when I get back, OK?"

"OK," she said.

"Let me see the ring," he said.

Barbara reached down into her neckline and pulled out a white gold ring set with a ten-millimeter Tahitian pearl.

The ring had arrived for her at work last Valentine's day, along with a dozen roses. She told him she didn't wear it on her hand because she had to wear gloves all the time. And that was true to a point—that's why she didn't wear it at work. But that's not why she didn't wear it when she got home from work.

She held the ring near her face so Arthur could see it in the laptop camera. He smiled like she'd just said she'd marry him.

He'd already asked her to, but she'd put him off. She knew she'd have to decide. Sometime around New Year's.

"You look good," she said to him, taking in his bright green eyes that didn't lose a bit of their glimmer across thousands of miles of transmission.

"You look perfect," he said, reaching out to touch the screen again.

Barbara was glad she'd taken time to cry that morning before she'd gotten out of bed.

ৡৡ

At the end of her shift, Barbara grabbed her big down coat from her locker and made sure her car keys and wallet were in the pockets. Then she made her way to the elevators.

As she stepped on the elevator, a voice called out, "Can you hold it?" She reached her hand instinctively to hold open the door. As soon as she processed whom the voice belonged to, she regretted her decision. She met the other resident's eyes and considered leaping off the elevator to take the stairs. Then the doors shut, and it was too late.

"I'm Chris," he said.

"Hi Chris." She kept her eyes on the metal doors in front of her.

"You're Barbara."

She turned and frowned at him. *Creep*, she told him with her eyes.

"My best friend around here is Morgan," he said. "His wife is Donna. She graduated from your program last year."

"Oh," Barbara said. Donna was her best friend.

"I'm Chris," he said again, this time holding out his hand.

"Barbara," she said, shaking it.

"I'm in the sports program with Morgan. But you probably just figured that out."

She took in his tall build, his broad shoulders. *Definitely a jock doc*, she thought.

"So here's the thing," he continued, as though they were carrying on a normal, two-person conversation. "I can't think of a single reason why you shouldn't go out with me on Friday night."

Barbara felt panic take hold in her gut. She tried to keep it off of her face but was pretty sure she failed. "Like a date?"

"Like dinner. I'll pick you up."

She thought quickly. She had to get away from this man, right now. What would do the trick?

"OK," she said.

"OK?" he said. "Really?"

"I said *OK*," she snapped.

The elevator doors opened.

"Can I have your number so we can hammer out the details?"

Barbara took off through the doors, heading for the sky bridge. Over her shoulder she shouted, "Get it from Donna!" Then she burst through the glass doors into the cold.

❧

She didn't see Chris the entire next day. She avoided any place he might be: the cafeteria, the coffee shop, even the elevators. She took the stairs everywhere. She even discovered two hospital staircases she hadn't known existed. She stuck to the dermatology clinic as much as possible, and then rushed home, keeping her head down. She even wore a hat to hide her bright blond hair.

But then, while she was driving home, her phone rang. She pressed the button on the steering wheel to answer it.

"Hello?"

"Barbara! It's Chris. I'm calling to get your address for our date tomorrow."

"Tomorrow?"

"Tomorrow is Friday."

"Right. I lost track of the days. You know how it is."

"I do, actually."

I can't do this. I can't do this, Barbara thought. *I can't.*

"So," he said. "Can I have your address?"

"Um." She had to stall. How could she stall? "Can you send me an email? I'm driving right now, and it's easier for me to give you directions if I can email you. Donna has my email address."

She could tell him to leave her alone in an email. It would be easy.

"Sure thing," he said, and he hung up.

But when Barbara got home and opened her laptop on the kitchen counter, there wasn't an email from Chris waiting for her. There was an email from Donna.

Chris is actually really great, Barbara, Donna wrote. *I know how hard this must be for you, but maybe one dinner would be good for you. If there were one guy in the whole hospital I'd pick—well, besides Morgan—I'd pick him.*

I'd pick him, Donna had written.

I'd pick him.

But Barbara had already picked. She'd picked Bob, and now Bob was dead.

This wasn't going to work.

Suddenly, Barbara was furious. She was furious that Chris had used Donna to push his way into her life, and that Donna had let herself be used.

She picked up her phone, clicked the last number on her call list and waited for him to answer, drumming her fingers on the kitchen counter.

"Hey Barbara," Chris said, picking up after one ring.

"So, you had Donna do your dirty work?"

"What?"

"I got home and thought there'd be an email from you. Instead there's an email from Donna telling me to go out with you."

"You think I did that?"

"Wouldn't you think so?"

"Can anyone *make* Donna do anything? I thought you guys were friends."

Barbara paused a moment. It was true. You could crack granite off of Donna's attitude.

"You didn't tell her to help you out?"

"No way. I haven't even called her yet to get your email address. Hang up with me and call her if you want to check."

"I believe you," she said.

It was a strange feeling, trusting someone new.

Chris paused. "Thank you," he said.

"Do you have a pen?" Barbara asked.

ℛ

Friday night, Chris pulled up in front of Barbara's apartment. She lived in a two-story townhouse—not an apartment at all, by Chris' standards—located in a cozy little neighborhood filled with young families and few students. He pulled into her driveway and parked next to her car. Even though it was dark out, the red color screamed in the dim streetlights.

He climbed the brick porch steps, taking in the large flower pots—empty of all but dirt—wondering what she would plant in them once it grew warm again.

He rang her doorbell.

A few moments later she answered. She wore a dark red dress that fell to her knees, some sort of strappy shoes that made her ankles look impossibly tiny, and a necklace with a giant pearl ring on it. He took her down coat from her hands and held it for her to put on. Mostly he wanted an excuse to get close to her to see if she smelled as fine as she looked.

She did.

As she slipped her right arm into her sleeve, he noticed a tattoo on her forearm.

"Wait," he said. "Can I see that?"

"Sure, OK," she said, holding out her arm.

He held her wrist in both of his hands. The tattoo wasn't small, nothing silly like some of the other girl residents had, little flowers on their ankles or hidden on their shoulders. This tattoo was bold and dark, two creatures curving toward one another, nearly forming a heart. Their bodies entwined at the bottom in some complicated fashion that he couldn't fathom. It was really the last thing he expected to find on her.

He was utterly fascinated.

"I'm guessing there's a story there."

"Sure is."

"You'll probably tell me when you're ready."

She slipped her arm into the sleeve of her coat and turned to face him, zipping up.

"Maybe."

They stepped out the door, and she turned to lock up.

Chris faced the two vehicles in the driveway. There was his truck with no heat. He exhaled, watching his breath mist in front of him. *It must be twenty-five degrees out here tonight*, he thought. Then there was her obviously brand-new car.

It was time to swallow his pride.

"Do you mind if we take your car?" he asked.

"What?" she said, her voice rising as though she were suddenly angry about something. Chris couldn't imagine what he'd done now.

"I don't have any heat in my truck."

"I'm driving."

"That's fine," he said in a gentling tone.

She ignored the arm he offered her and stomped down the stairs to the driver's side door, shattering any doubts he might have had about her ability to get around in heels.

When they climbed in, the car was already running—she'd started it from her keychain somehow. But the car had been so quiet he'd barely heard it.

"Is this one of those electric cars?" he asked.

"It's a Tesla."

"So it doesn't go very fast then?"

"Are you serious?"

Barbara rolled her eyes so hard it looked like it might have hurt. She reversed out of the driveway, then headed up her residential street at a sedate pace. But then she hit the traffic circle like an F1 racer wending through a chicane (Chris liked his racing), turned left at the next light onto the bypass and took off like a shot. She kept her hands at three and nine—racing position—and never moved them from the wheel, even when turning.

If he thought he couldn't take his eyes off of her while she strolled around the hospital, he was riveted while watching her drive.

Nice wheels indeed.

In a blink they arrived at the restaurant, a storefront with street parking, and she parallel parked so quickly, so perfectly—of *course* she did—that it didn't seem she even needed to look at what she was doing after the initial glance over her shoulder.

Once the keys were in her hand again, Chris leaned

his head back in his seat.

"Wow," he said. "Who taught you to drive?"

"What?"

"I asked you, Who—"

"No, never mind." She jumped out of the car and slammed the door. She was already inside the restaurant while he was still climbing out of the car.

He entered the restaurant behind her, pretending nothing was wrong, and waited with her for the host.

The restaurant was his favorite, one that the students shunned, with white linen tablecloths and not a pool table in sight. The bartender, Justin, was one of his roommates, and Chris nodded to him. The bar ran along the right wall the entire back half of the place, while the front half was reserved for dining. They served a mix of southern and French food, and if Chris closed his eyes, it almost tasted like home.

"Bouchard. Party of two," he told the host.

The host showed them to their table, and handed Chris the wine list. Chris immediately set down the list and looked at Barbara.

"We don't have to do this. I promise. I won't ever talk to you again if you don't want me to."

She just stared at her water glass.

"I can't drag you through a meal if you're going to be miserable. You've been miserable since we left your house."

She looked up, her green eyes flashing now. "I wasn't miserable. I was pissed off at you."

Chris raised his eyebrows. "You sure that's all it was?"

"You insulted my car."

"I sure did. It was an accident."

Barbara crossed her arms over her chest.

"Do you really care about that though? Seems pretty silly."

She was staring at her water glass again. Chris decided that faking through a terrible dinner wasn't going to get him any closer to her. But speaking some truth might. So he went after the truth even if it meant he'd lose her.

"Here's what I think. I asked you about that gorgeous mark on your arm, and it meant something more to you than you let on. And then I said something stupid that did more than insult your car, it insulted you in some way, I just don't know how. And then, after you drove us here like you belong on a track rather than in a medical program, I asked you where you learned to drive like that, and you froze me out worse than you have all night."

Chris leaned forward.

"I think all of those things have something to do with that pearl ring around your neck."

Barbara reached up and grabbed the ring, as though she'd forgotten she was wearing it.

"My husband died," she said. "No one here knows."

"He gave you that ring?"

"No," she said. "It's from someone else."

"Your husband teach you to drive?"

"Yeah. He was a pilot, but he also liked his cars."

"He did a good job."

Barbara laughed, covering her mouth to stifle the noise. "Thank you," she said, after calming down. "He always thought I needed to practice more. He'd take me to the tracks for my birthday."

"He bought you the car?"

"In a way."

Chris was getting used to her half-answers, so he let that one go.

"Hey Snake," Justin said, walking up to the table with a bottle of champagne.

"Justin, this is Barbara."

"Compliments of the house," Justin said, popping the cork and filling two flutes.

As he walked back to the bar, Barbara's back to him, Justin mouthed, "GOOD GOD" and pointed at her. Chris gave him a look that could melt paint.

"A friend of yours?"

"A roommate."

"Really? I thought all the jock docs lived together. Except for Morgan of course."

"Not all of us."

She picked up her glass. "Cheers."

They clinked glasses.

"So why did he call you 'Snake'? That's a weird nickname."

Chris laughed. "It's a basketball thing. We all have our nicknames. That one's mine."

"Is there a story behind it?"

"Sure is."

She stared at him, her gray-green eyes open wide. Then she laughed again, and it was the greatest sound he'd ever heard in his life.

"How about this," he said. "I'll tell you something I wouldn't want anyone to know. Then you tell me something you wouldn't want anyone to know."

"Blackmail-as-trust?" she said, with the sexiest half-smile.

"Call it what you like."

"OK. You first."

Chris decided on a full-court-press. "I grew up in a single-wide trailer on the Texas side of the Louisiana-Texas border, right where the river hits the Gulf. Our town mostly got washed away after Hurricane Rita back in 2005. My aunt and her baby died in that flood. So did my dad, trying to save them."

Barbara sat back hard in her chair, her mouth open slightly.

"I don't have much in the way of money. Can't fix my truck right now." He tipped his glass at her. "Thanks for driving."

"I'm so sorry your dad died. You must have been young. Sixteen?"

"Seventeen."

"What about the rest of your family?"

"I have a mom and two little sisters. We make do."

"You support them."

He nodded.

"That'll be easier come May when your program's over."

He nodded again. "Your turn," he said.

"I got married my second year of medical school, when I was twenty-three, to this guy I'd grown up with from my old neighborhood. He was just two years out of the Air Force Academy. Flying missions in Afghanistan and Pakistan. Honestly, I don't really know what he did over there. I wasn't allowed to know.

"About three weeks before he was supposed to come home on leave, a chaplain showed up at my apartment. I was a war widow at twenty-five. That was three years ago." Saying the words, Barbara was amazed by how ordinary the story sounded. How run-of-the-mill. She got married, and her husband died. It happened all the time. She was nothing special. She was fine, in fact. A doctor. In one more year, she'd be a dermatologist, able to make a killer living. She was *just fine*.

So why wasn't she fine?

Chris slowly reached across the table and picked up her hand as though her bones might break under his touch. She marveled at his giant hands. *Snake*, she thought, *a basketball nickname*. These hands were used to doing things, not small delicate maneuvers, but big, strong, powerful things.

"I want to come to one of the jock doc games," she

said.

"Do you want to come this Sunday? We play at four."

"Sure. Do you—" She looked at her own tiny hand, resting in his, suddenly feeling shy. "Do you want me to pick you up?"

⥤⥢

Barbara pulled her car into the gravel driveway of the shabby bungalow. She knew lots of undergraduates lived in houses like this, but she didn't realize any of her colleagues did. She bet Chris' colleagues didn't realize he lived in a place like this, either. She started to wonder if maybe she and Chris weren't such a terrible match after all.

Chris opened the door to his place before she could even turn off her engine. He was wearing shorts despite the freezing weather, along with a warm coat. He carried a basketball under one arm and a pair of shoes under the other.

"I turned the heat up for you," she said, once he closed the door.

"Feels awesome." He reached behind him and placed the ball and shoes in the back seat.

"What's with the two pairs of shoes?"

"Girl, you don't wear your court shoes anyplace but on the court. I see your education needs to start now."

While she drove them to the rec center north of campus, Chris gave her some basketball basics. She also learned he had played in college—which she knew was impressive—and that he refused to play if Morgan wasn't on his team.

"A big man is nothing without his point guard. And Morgan's the only point guard worth a damn."

"They want you to play badly enough to give you

your way on this?"

Chris just chuckled.

OK, Barbara thought. *So he's a little cocky.*

She followed him through the propped-open double doors to the gymnasium. Squeaks of sneakers and shouting of voices rang out before she set her eyes on the court, where a group of nine or ten other sports fellows were warming up—some shooting baskets alone, some guarding each other in a casual way.

"Barbara!" Donna called out from the bleachers, where she sat, her braids pulled up in a bun, her new baby girl asleep in a sling across her chest.

"Good luck," she said to Chris.

He gave her a big smile and held out the basketball to her. "Just touch it. For luck."

"Don't be ridiculous." But she tapped the basketball with two fingers before climbing up the bleachers to join Donna.

∽✍

Chris changed his shoes, then stepped onto the court. He dribbled twice and then pulled up into a jump shot, *swish*. Morgan was there, and he sent the ball back to Chris with a laser-sharp pass before trotting over to Chris' side.

"Guess things went well at dinner," Morgan said.

"Guess they did." Chris pulled up again. *Swish*. He smiled.

"Donna says Barbara won't tell her anything either."

"Barbara and I have an understanding."

"Aw man. Give me something!" Morgan said.

Chris grabbed the ball and turned toward his best friend, whispering, "OK. How's this for something? I'm going to marry that girl."

"What?"

Chris just laughed and dribbled away.

At that point, Jericho faced-up against Chris on defense. Chris picked up the ball into an easy three-point position.

"I saw who you came in here with," Jericho said. "You hit that?"

"Shut up, Jerry."

Chris pump-faked, watched Jericho leave his feet, then drop-stepped past him and dunked.

Morgan hooted, then clapped his hands. "Time to team up, people. Who's the other captain this week?"

Barbara watched the men split into two teams through some complicated process that involved both history of past won games and the making of free throws. Just like Chris had told her, he and Morgan were on the same team. After a few minutes, it was time for the game to start.

That's when Barbara noticed Donna had a stopwatch. "Really?" Barbara asked her. "You're the time-keeper?"

"And de facto scorekeeper if there's a dispute," she said, pointing at a clipboard at her feet. "But it would be great if you could do that for me. One point per basket, no matter where they hit it from."

Barbara picked up the clipboard and the pencil resting on it. She drew two columns, then wrote "Snake" at the top of one and "Jerry" at the top of the other. She laughed to herself at the name Chris had called the sports fellow Jericho, a guy she'd never, ever liked.

Last spring, maybe six months ago, Jericho had asked her out. They'd been in line for coffee one morning, and she'd felt his eyes on her, as though her scrubs were see-through. Men like Jericho made her wonder if she would ever meet another man as good as Bob again.

She ordered her coffee, but before she could pull out her card to pay, he slipped his own across the counter.

"You're Barbara, right?" he said, handing her the coffee.

"Yes."

"I'm Jericho."

"Thanks for the coffee." She turned to leave.

"Hey, wait a minute," he called after her, running to catch up, losing his own place in line. "Wanna hang out some time?"

"I can't. I'm engaged." She pulled the ring out from inside her scrubs.

"That's not a diamond."

She tilted her head, her eyes saying, *Really, asshole?*

"I'm just saying. I'd buy a girl like you a diamond."

"See you around, Jericho." She turned to leave, but not before she heard him whisper *bitch* under his breath as she walked away.

৽৽৶

All of the guys seemed to be very good basketball players. But Chris—and Morgan—were exceptional. She realized Chris hadn't been cocky at all earlier. He was clearly the best player on the court. Even her untrained eye could see that.

But he was right—he really relied on Morgan to get him the ball. Morgan's passes made Chris a better player. She liked that about him. He recognized a good teammate, and he wanted that teammate around. Those were her values too.

She looked down at her score sheet. Chris' team was up by five points. "How much time is left, Donna?"

"A little over two minutes. Hang on—TWO MINUTES!" she bellowed to the guys on the court.

"Time out!" yelled Jericho.

"What for?" Morgan asked.

"Score check," Jericho said, looking at Barbara and her clipboard.

"It's twenty-three to eighteen," Barbara said.

"Bullshit!" Jericho said to her. "We have nineteen."

"You have eighteen," Chris said, looking at Jericho's teammates. Barbara thought they looked uneasy.

"No we don't," said Jericho. "We have nineteen."

"Fine, OK. You have nineteen," Chris said.

"I want to know why our scorekeeper is trying to cheat us out of a point, and why you're protecting her."

"Shut up, Jericho," Morgan said.

"Yeah, man. No one's cheating anybody," said another guy, this one on Jericho's own team.

"Chris is protecting that cheating bitch—" Jericho pointed a finger at Barbara, "—because he's schtupping her. That's the only reason."

Barbara stood, her face burning, the clipboard and pencil dropping to the floor beneath the bleachers. As shouting voices broke out, she ran from the gym.

§∞§

Chris watched Barbara leave, and every part of him wanted to run after her.

But he couldn't, not yet. He walked up to Jericho. Jericho pulled back his shoulders and tilted up his chin, hoping to gain an extra inch or two. Chris had seen it before in guys he'd faced off with in the trailer park growing up.

Chris spoke quietly. "You know I could drop you here."

"I'd like to see you—" Jericho spoke loud enough for others to hear.

"Just admit it to yourself," Chris said, his voice

pitched at a near-whisper. "You'd be in pieces. I want you to know it. I want you to know that I'm choosing not to do it."

With that he walked by Morgan and squeezed his friend's shoulder, and Morgan nodded back. Only then did he walk off the court, already planning how to make things right with Barbara.

Someone on the other team yelled "Forfeit!" but Morgan replied, "This is not a forfeit. This is a draw."

ৎৎৎ

After fleeing the gym, Barbara drove straight home, weeping in her car, then dragged herself into bed. She stayed there until her phone rang. Donna.

"What," she said.

"Jericho is such a jerk! I can't believe he—"

"I don't care about Jericho."

Donna was quiet for a minute. "We're heading home from the gym now. It took us a minute to gather up our gear and get the princess loaded in the car. But Chris left as soon as you did."

"He did?"

"He seemed pretty upset by what happened."

"He did?"

"But I think he had to take the bus though."

"Oh! I drove him there. I can't believe I left him."

"I think he'll forgive you," Donna said. "Really, he's probably less upset about having to take the bus than he is about not getting his free coffee next week." Donna explained the coffee wager. "I know Morgan is already annoyed to have to buy his own."

Barbara laughed. "Coffee is indeed the true tragedy here."

After hanging up with Donna, Barbara jumped from her bed and threw on clothes. She sped over to the hospital and parked in the deck. She ran over the bridge, through the doors and down the stairs to the coffee shop. On a Sunday afternoon, the line was mercifully short. She bought a twenty dollar gift card and tucked it in her wallet.

∽∾

After changing his shoes and grabbing his ball, Chris waited at the bus stop outside the rec center. He rode the bus home, then showered and changed. After that, he started pacing. His long legs took him back and forth across his living and dining rooms quickly, even factoring in the detour around the foosball table.

Justin sat on the couch drinking a beer.

"You should go over there," Justin said.

"Just show up?"

"If you call first, she might tell you not to come."

"Isn't the whole point to not be an ass? You know, to let her have a say in the matter?"

"Sure, but gestures are nice, too."

"Gestures, huh."

Justin lifted his beer.

"I cannot believe I'm taking advice from you."

"Dude, I am a bartender."

Chris ran out the door and hopped in his truck.

∽∾

Barbara was sitting at her kitchen table. It was a lovely table, a heavy butcher block crafted of golden maple, seated upon trestle legs. It looked like it could withstand a hurricane.

At the thought of hurricanes, she remembered Chris' family, the drowning and death.

She stared at her cell phone where it sat in the middle

of the table, deciding what to do. Next to the phone was the coffee shop gift card.

Knock-knock.

Startled, she jumped to her feet, slipping on the oak floors in her ankle socks. She grabbed the table to steady herself.

"Hello?" she called.

"Barbara? Hey. It's Chris. I hope you don't mind me—" he stopped, and then she heard some muffled words that sounded like, *Aw heck.*

She opened the door. He stood there wearing jeans and a snap-up cowboy shirt over a dark blue undershirt. His black hair was still damp from the shower, his brown eyes uncertain. His wool peacoat was unbuttoned, like he'd left in a hurry, and he held his leather gloves in his hands.

He looked nothing like Bob, Bob with his dark blond hair and crystal blue eyes. But he was handsome. It was an undeniable fact.

"Come in," she said.

She let him lead the way into her place and admired his broad shoulders from behind. She found herself wanting to touch him.

Having him in her place, she almost lost her nerve. She needed something to do, to say.

The gift card.

"Donna called me," she said, leading him into the kitchen. "She told me you walked off the court after I left."

"Yeah."

"She also told me about the coffee wager."

Chris laughed. "We didn't lose, if you're worried about that. The game was declared a draw."

"But you did lose your free coffee because of me." She picked up the coffee card and placed it in his hand. "To keep you warm this week."

Chris opened his hand and saw the coffee card. He stared at it for a moment, trying to figure out when Barbara would have found the time to get it for him between leaving the gym and now. Then he tucked it in his pocket. He wanted both hands free so he could pull her closer to him, just a little bit. He leaned down, as slowly as he could possibly move, giving her every chance to pull away. Then he placed his lips on hers.

❦

The next morning, Barbara picked up Chris from his bungalow so they could carpool to work.

When she chatted with Arthur on Wednesday, she didn't mention Chris to him at all.

By Friday, his toothbrush was by her sink.

She didn't mention Chris to Arthur the following Wednesday, either, even though by then, Chris was living in his bungalow in name only, and his truck was more often than not parked in her driveway next to her red car.

Three Weeks Until Christmas

One night in early December, Chris and Barbara were walking home to her apartment from a nearby restaurant. They'd been having drinks and snacks after work. They strolled along the sidewalk, the storefront restaurants and bars glowing with warmth. Each lamppost was decorated with a two-foot round lighted snowflake. When you looked all the way down the street, the town looked like a twinkling fairyland.

One of the reasons Barbara picked her apartment was that—even though she loved to drive her car—she loved being able to walk places. She missed the urban life of Boston.

She shoved aside thoughts of Boston.

Up ahead, she saw a familiar face—Tripp, another guy who lived in her apartment complex. Tripp was an MBA student, set to graduate that spring. Tripp was friendly enough, but when they'd first gotten to know each other, she'd had to fend him off too.

"Hey Barbara," Tripp said, eying her hand that was interlaced with Chris'. Suddenly nervous, Barbara dropped Chris' hand.

"Chris, this is Tripp, my neighbor."

"Nice to meet you," Chris said.

Tripp didn't say anything, but he looked confused, and angry too. He grabbed her arm, pulling her to the side. "Who is this guy, Barb? I thought you were engaged to Arthur."

"Let go of my arm, Tripp."

"You're making a mistake."

"If I am, then it's my mistake." Barbara looked at Chris over her shoulder. He was standing just behind her, his arms hanging by his sides. She realized maybe his name *Snake* meant something else entirely, something that could be dangerous.

"This is how it is?" Tripp demanded.

"If you mean that I'm not ever going to go out with you, then yes. This is how it is." She yanked her arm free. "And don't manhandle people."

"I didn't—"

"Yes, you did." She pointed at her arm.

Tripp stepped back, embarrassed. "I'm sorry."

"Don't be sorry. Be better." She laced her fingers into Chris' again. "Good night, Tripp."

They walked on, and once the stress of the confrontation wore off, Barbara felt anxious. She had another secret she needed to tell Chris.

"Arthur is the guy who gave me the ring."

"OK." Chris seemed cool, like nothing at all had happened a few moments ago.

"He's deployed right now."

Chris nodded.

"He was Bob's best friend. Now we chat every week. He thinks he wants to marry me."

"Do you want to marry him?"

"No."

"Well then," Chris said, pulling Barbara's hand to his mouth and kissing the back of it. "That's all that matters."

Barbara felt an unexpected wave of relief. Another secret released into the cool night sky.

"Thank you," she said.

"For what?"

"For letting me fight my own fight back there."

"You didn't need rescuing."

Barbara thought about all the family she'd left behind in Boston. "I wish everybody felt that way."

Two Weeks Until Christmas

Barbara knew it was time to tell Arthur about Chris. Three Wednesdays had passed without a word from her about him, and the guilt was killing her. Now, the second Wednesday in December, she would let him know. It was a terrible thing to do, to ruin his Christmas like this, but she had to tell him the truth.

She sat on the break room cot and logged on. She waited and waited. Finally, a face appeared. Marty, Arthur's friend, another classmate from the Academy. He looked grim.

"Where's Arthur, Marty?" she asked.

"He's gone, Barbara," he said. "There was a fuel fire. We think it was sabotage. It's still being investigated."

Barbara looked up from the computer, staring at the wooden door in front of her.

He's gone.

Marty was still talking. "I'm not even supposed to tell you this much, since you weren't married yet and all, but I thought you deserved to know."

Barbara left her laptop and headphones on the bed and ran from the room. As she ran, she pulled her cell phone from her pocket and dialed a number. She ran and ran, through the main atrium, out of the hospital, into the freezing cold without her coat, all the way up the hill to Franklin Street, the main road through town. By the time she got there, sweating and shivering, Donna was pulling up in her car, wearing her white coat from work over a dress and comfortable heels.

Only after Donna pulled away from the curb did Barbara start sobbing. "He's dead," she said. "He's dead. He died, Donna!"

Donna drove toward Barbara's apartment.

"I don't want to go home!" Barbara screamed. "I can't."

"OK," said Donna, soothing, the way she talked to her baby daughter. "Let me get some of your things, and you can stay at our house."

Barbara waited in Donna's car while Donna packed a bag. While she waited, she pictured Arthur's bright green eyes, sparkling on the laptop screen, except the green kept turning blue. She couldn't keep the colors straight.

༺ঌয়༻

Barbara awoke in Donna and Morgan's guest room later that evening. She was still in her scrubs from work. She stood and ripped them from her body. Then she hopped in the shower, scalding herself until her skin turned red like a turnip.

She climbed out and pulled on the pajamas Donna had packed for her. She wandered out into the house. She heard voices in the living room, but they stopped when she entered the room. Morgan and Donna sat on the couch.

"I drove your car home from the hospital," Morgan said. "That thing is sweet."

Barbara felt her face crumple again, as Donna whacked her husband on the shoulder.

"No," she said, trying to keep it together. "It's OK. He's right. It is sweet." She smiled at Morgan, sitting in one of the chairs that surrounded the coffee table. "I called you guys because there's no one else I can talk to about Arthur dying. No one else understands what's going on."

Donna and Morgan eyed each other.

"I mean, when Bob died, I thought I would never figure out how to go on. This isn't like that. Arthur wasn't the center of my world. But Arthur dying definitely showed me I'm not ready to move past Bob's death yet."

"How's that?" Donna asked.

"I just feel so—so guilty. I've never felt guilt like this before in my life. It's unbearable."

Donna spoke with hesitation. "What do you feel guilty for?"

"For tricking Arthur! For—for thinking someone could ever be as good as Bob! God! Don't you see?"

Donna and Morgan looked at each other again.

"Why do you two keep doing that?" Barbara demanded.

"What about Chris?" Morgan asked.

"That's clearly over!" Barbara was shouting now, and hoped she wouldn't wake the baby. But she had to make them see.

"Because he's not as good as Bob?" Donna asked.

"Of course not! No one will ever be as good as Bob!"

"Never?"

"Arg!" Barbara yelled, standing. "I'm going back to bed."

ও๑

For a week, Barbara dodged Chris at the hospital. She used her secret stairwells. She arrived early and stayed late, hoping her odd hours would work in her favor. Strangely, though, it seemed he was avoiding her as well.

One time she saw Jericho from a distance, but he quickly averted his eyes, as though she were a light too bright to look at.

That's weird, she thought.

She did her job and then went home to Donna's house. She couldn't go to her own apartment. Chris lived there now, and she didn't know how to kick him out.

She needed a way to get her home back without having to see him. She didn't know what would happen if she had to see him. All she knew was that she was afraid.

She wished she could go back in time to that moment in the elevator, before he spoke to her, and redirect her entire future.

One Week Until Christmas

The Wednesday before Christmas, Barbara's day felt empty. There would be no call to Arthur today. There would be no more calls to him at all.

The hospital's holiday decorations mocked her with their expressions of joy. The nurses' stations were decorated with garlands of tinsel and holly. Twinkling lights hung in the main atrium near the coffee shop—which meant she couldn't avoid them. And next to the coffee shop stood a breathtakingly tall Christmas tree, fifteen, maybe twenty feet in height, topped with an angel that looked oddly like a pagan fairy. Even the music piped into the public spaces was all holiday tunes now, rather than unobtrusive muzak. Ordinarily, she would enjoy it all.

But now, she couldn't. She was more alone than she had been when she first arrived. Back then, she was just a widow. Now she was not only a widow, she was a betrayer, and capricious, too.

She could barely stand herself.

She found herself outside the break room where she'd made her calls to Arthur, and she was glad of it, because she began to cry again. She ducked through the door.

Down the hall, Chris watched Barbara, his strong and precious love, fall to pieces and enter the break room. He'd stayed out of her way this past week, getting updates from Morgan. But this, seeing her like this, he couldn't take it any more. He knew a thing or two about grieving, and he knew doing it alone wasn't the right way.

He knocked on the break room door.

"Yes? Um, come in!" she called out.

He opened the door and shut it behind him. She sat on a cot, back stiff, as though nothing were wrong. But when she saw it was him, she stood, angry, their toes almost touching in the tiny room.

"What are you doing in here?"

"I saw you."

"You saw me?"

"Yep. And I want to tell you a story."

"A *story*?"

"Yep. A Christmas story."

She plopped back down on the cot. "Fine. Tell me a Christmas story."

Chris swallowed his smile, and sat on the cot next to her, giving her plenty of room.

"After my mom's sister, her baby and my dad died in Rita's flood, we didn't know how to come back to happy after that. My uncle and my mom, they were both wrecks. Where I come from, when people lose everything, they turn to drinking and other dangerous things."

"This is a Christmas story?"

"Sure is."

"Fine. Go on."

Chris nodded. "It seemed like no time passed at all and then it was Christmas time. My two little sisters, they still wanted Christmas. Back then, they were only eight and ten. So I went to my mom's other sister, Patty, and I told her about needing to have Christmas at our house— man." He laughed, interrupting himself. "Just telling this story I sound like I just came out of the swamp."

"Actually," Barbara said. "You sound great."

Chris looked at her, seeing the smile lines around her eyes, and felt hopeful. He picked up her hand. "It wasn't easy. Patty came over to our place, where my mom was barely hanging on and only for my little sisters' sakes. My uncle, Stevie, he was living in my bedroom. I was sleeping on the couch. Since I was leaving for college in a few months, and Stevie was homeless, it seemed like an OK situation for everybody."

"What did Patty do?"

"She brought her record player and her cookbook and just started cooking. She cooked to Christmas music all day and all night. She invited everyone over, all the time—well, not the ones cooking meth, but they wouldn't have come anyway. But all our family, and all our friends, they came over to eat Patty's neverending supply of food off our picnic table. My mom would get exasperated, saying, 'Patty, where you getting money to feed the whole town?' Patty would just laugh."

"Where did she get the money?"

"Later, I figured out people were slipping her money to buy the food so she could keep cooking. Then these same people would come for dinner every night to keep my mom and uncle company. Soon, Stevie took up a spot at that picnic table and talked to everyone who came by, listening to beautiful stories about his wife, about how gorgeous his baby girl had been. And he cried a lot, but he got to hear those stories too, so it was worth it."

At this point, Chris saw that Barbara was crying. He squeezed her hand tighter.

"And my mom, even though she complained, she had people at her house day and night, and one of them brought a Christmas tree, and then one of them brought some lights and hung them around the trailer the way my dad used to. And one brought this crazy inflatable plastic Santa for the yard that my sisters just loved." Chris realized he was crying too. "The point is, Patty and all of the people who came, they didn't let my mom and uncle be. They loved them back to life."

Barbara reached around behind her neck and unhooked the clasp on the chain holding the pearl ring to her body.

"What should I do with this?" she asked him, lowering the ring and chain into his hand.

Chris hefted the ring, then admired it.

"This is really beautiful."

"Yeah," Barbara said. "Thanks."

"Do you think we should save it for our daughters?"

Christmas Present

"I have always thought of Christmas time…as a good time; a kind, forgiving, charitable, pleasant time; the only time I know of, in the long calendar of the year, when men and women seem by one consent to open their shut-up hearts freely, and to think of people below them as if they really were fellow-passengers to the grave, and not another race of creatures bound on other journeys."
— Charles Dickens, *A Christmas Carol*

Noëlle

Cheryl McAlister

"It's for a full year," Dan said. "You sure you want this place?" He took off his reading glasses and handed the lease back to the landlord.

"I have to stay in Paris," David answered, "and I can't find a rent this low anywhere else." He and Pascal were poking around the little apartment. It needed painting. The tall windows that opened onto the street were filthy, but they would let in plenty of light. Pascal looked into the WC. The old fashioned tank was mounted high on the wall and flushed with a pull chain. "Your knees will keep the door from closing when you sit," he complained.

"That's all right. I'll be alone. I'll leave it open."

David opened another door to what must have been a closet at one time. It held a narrow pre-fab shower with a high step into it. Beside the shower were a small sink and some raw plywood shelves.

Monsieur Hamidou said something in French to Pascal who translated for David. "He says the shower is new. The last tenant installed it."

"Tell him I'll paint the place if he'll provide a few gallons."

"Liters," Pascal corrected.

"You know what I mean."

Pascal huffed and translated.

Monsieur Hamidou considered for a moment before answering.

"What did he say?"

"He says he likes artists, and since you're an artist, you can paint the walls."

"I'm not going to paint a mural. He gets that, right? I just want white paint." Most of the buildings on the street below were covered with murals and graffiti.

Monsieur Hamidou nodded and said, "Yes, OK, paint." He smiled broadly as he pushed a pen and two copies of the lease toward David. "Very good," he said. "You write?"

"Look OK?" David asked.

Dan shrugged. "It's a standard lease."

David signed both copies and handed them back to Monsieur Hamidou who signed, then stood looking expectantly at the three men.

David understood, took out his wallet, and counted out the euros for one month's rent plus security deposit. Monsieur Hamidou furrowed his brow, smoothed his mustache and re-counted the bills, occasionally turning them to face the same direction.

"Really?" David muttered.

But the landlord was smiling again and said, "*Très bien*. Welcome Mr. Glaser." He pocketed the money and his copy of the lease, and gave David a key ring.

"The little one's the mailbox," Dan translated. "The round one is for the entry, and that one's for the apartment door."

Monsieur Hamidou continued chatting with Dan and Pascal. Finally, after what seemed to David like forever, he looked at his watch, said, "*Bonsoir*" and shook hands all around.

"So when do you want to move in?" Dan asked after he left.

"Soon as possible."

"Is Brooke pressuring you to leave?" asked Pascal.

"Not really. She's not even there. She's been staying with the new guy, but I gotta get out soon. That apartment belongs to her father."

"We wondered how you two could afford to live there, but Dan wouldn't let me ask."

Dan took Pascal by the arm. "Because you're too nosy. Come on, let's walk down to La Veilleuse and grab an *apéro* to celebrate David's new digs."

It was five-thirty, and the late-August heat was finally lifting. The café wasn't busy; most Parisians were on vacation, so David and Dan laughed when Pascal rushed to claim a sidewalk table as if it were the last one on Earth.

"What's so funny?" he asked.

"Seriously?" said David. It felt good to laugh.

Brooke had introduced David to Pascal and Dan five years before, and the couples had grown close. Back then, Pascal was Adella's lead ready-to-wear designer and had hired Brooke as his assistant. When Pascal left Adella to start his own label, he made sure Brooke got his position.

"Have you seen her?" David asked impulsively. He had promised himself he wouldn't.

"Not at all," said Dan. "What happened?"

"Fuck if I know. She came home last Tuesday and said she met someone else. Said I was holding her back, and she was sick of me relying on her for everything."

"What does that mean?"

"For one thing, she didn't want to translate any more so when we went out with clients or her boss I'd be stuck sitting there like an idiot." He took a sip of his beer then stared into the foam for a moment before adding, "It caused some pretty big fights."

"Why don't you just take French lessons?" Pascal asked.

"I have no ear for languages. Besides, why bother? It won't bring her back."

"It might if you made the effort."

"She's with someone else."

"*Bof*," Pascal scoffed. "She doesn't love him."

"How do you know?"

"It's too soon. It's just infatuation."

David hoped Pascal was right. He needed time to show Brooke he could get along fine without her. That should make her want him back.

"You want to borrow the car to move?" asked Dan.

"That would be great if I could drive."

"You don't have an international license?"

"I don't even have an American license."

"Why not?"

"The day before I was supposed to take the test my old man forced me to prove to him I could drive. This was after fifteen weeks of Driver's Ed and six months driving around with my mom. Anyway, he went ballistic when I let the clutch out too fast and stalled. Blasted me again for not turning around when I backed out. Then when I got to the stop sign at the end of our road he ripped me a new one for braking too hard. I was so pissed off I got out of the car and walked home. Never took the test; never drove again."

Pascal put his hand on David's arm. "My father is a—" He paused. "Daniel, *un connard?*"

"A bastard."

"My father is a bastard too." Pascal laughed. "*Voilà*, you see? Now you learn good French."

"Thanks, that'll come in handy."

"I studied your dad's buildings when I was in architecture school," Dan said.

"Oh, he's a brilliant designer, just an asshole."

"Does he at least like your work?" asked Pascal. "My father hates that I'm a couturier."

"Who knows? I've had work in *The New Yorker* and *Rolling Stone*, and I'm sure he's seen it, but he's never said anything, which is better than his usual response."

"What's that?"

"He'd tell me everything that was wrong with it... and me."

"But you're a very successful illustrator."

"Dan, if I ever told my father I illustrate covers for romance novels he'd freak out. He'd say I was a total failure even though I'm Pantaloon's primary illustrator."

"Will you tell him about Brooke?" Pascal asked.

"And bring up another failure?" David felt his throat tightening and took a swig of beer. "He gave me hell for following her here in the first place."

"He didn't like her?"

"He was crazy about her. Thought she was the perfect woman."

"Then what was the problem?"

"He didn't think I was good enough for her, and he wanted to save me the trouble of moving back. Said painting was the only thing I was good at, and other than that I'm spoiled and self-absorbed, and she'd leave me once she figured it out." David rubbed his eyes then smiled sardonically. "But he graciously admitted my shortcomings were his fault."

"People should be required to get a license to be a parent," said Dan. "We'll help you move. Can you wait till Sunday?"

‿◞◟‿

Monsieur Hamidou left a 2.5-liter can of white paint by the door. David wondered what he gave the last guy to install the shower, a spigot? But he couldn't ask for more even if he wanted to. Maybe he should take some French classes, but it would take forever to be able to ask for things like paint. It was easier to walk to the hardware store around the corner, grab the paint and plunk down some money.

After two days of painting, scrubbing and trying to sleep on a quilt on the floor, David's back ached. Thankfully, on the third day, Ikea delivered a chocolate brown futon, a laminated coffee table, a rattan rug and a pre-fab armoire. By the time he got the damned armoire together he was toast. He sprawled across the futon and surveyed his studio apartment. Besides his drawing table, flat file, and the table that held his computer and printer, all he brought from Brooke's apartment were his clothes, a box of art supplies, a quilt, a towel and his pillow. Maybe he should have taken the reading lamp and a few books too. He dialed her number.

She had a new phone message, in French, of course. David couldn't understand this one any better than the old one, but he could tell his name was no longer included. He hung up without leaving a message.

He opened the window and leaned out. Weird how his life could feel so over while the people on the street below went about theirs as usual: Two toddlers ran around their mothers' legs laughing, a couple of guys painted a new mural, and his landlord swept the sidewalk in front of the building. Must be nice to be so carefree.

He took a deep breath. This neighborhood was not only noisier than his old one in the sixteenth *arrondissement*, it was smellier. The reek of cigarettes and spray paint mixed with the aroma of Chinese food. David hadn't eaten much over the past week. Now the thought of Chinese take-out made his stomach growl. He decided to find the restaurant.

Monsieur Hamidou opened the street door for him when he returned with his bags of food. The jolly landlord, oblivious to David's inability to understand, began speaking rapidly. He took David by the elbow and led him to an apartment opposite the stairs in the courtyard. A plump, smiling woman wearing a green polka-dot dress and a pink flowered headscarf came to the door. Madame Hamidou. David shifted his bags to one arm to shake her hand.

"I'm sorry, I really don't understand a word you're saying," David said, but the Hamidous chattered away unconcerned. When they finally paused, he lifted his bags a little and nodded toward the stairs.

"*Allez, allez,*" said Madame Hamidou, and she turned him by the shoulders and shooed him off as if he had been the one keeping the conversation going.

It would have helped if he could have told them he had to leave, but he doubted he could ever learn to speak French. Still, it might impress Brooke. Back in his apartment he texted Dan to ask where he could find a class. "Nothing uptight," he wrote.

Dan texted back immediately, "This is where I went. Ten years ago, but they're still there. Good school. Glad you're doing this."

David took his box of fried rice to the computer to look up the school Dan recommended. Still no internet. He could find the website on his phone, but it would be much easier on the computer. Anyway, it didn't matter if he signed up now or next week. Brooke probably wouldn't care anyway; she was with someone else. And he was busy. He had to get going on the work he'd ignored since the break-up.

On top of his to-do list was Lilia Dufort's latest manuscript. The sketches were already a couple of days late, but he had to read the book before he could do the drawings. The last thing he was in the mood for was one of Dufort's ludicrous canned love stories, especially because for the last three years Brooke had been his model.

David spread the boxes of Chinese food on the coffee table and pulled the table close to the futon. He put his feet up and began reading *Foxglove and Foolscap*, by Lilia Dufort.

Her novels were so predictable he could get away with skimming through them. They were all set in France, so once he knew the time period and the hair and eye color of the current Aphrodite and Adonis he would get to work.

Not this time. *Foxglove and Foolscap* was about a beautiful, young wise-woman living in seventeenth century Paris who was accused of witchcraft and sentenced to burn at the stake. Dufort had developed her so convincingly, and the story was so intriguing, that David went back to re-read the parts he had skimmed. He began reading more slowly and found he couldn't put it down. By the time he finished the manuscript the next morning, he had fallen in love with the heroine, Noëlle.

Dufort described her as "petite and slender," with "ebony hair" and "fierce, ash-gray eyes." David rolled on his side and pictured how he'd compose the book cover. He'd portray Noëlle in a triumphant pose illuminated by flames with the duke in the background. He closed his eyes. He became the young nobleman saving her from the flames, then looking into those intense gray eyes as he let his fingertips wander over her silky skin...

For a moment, Brooke appeared as his model. He mentally pushed her away. His Noëlle would look nothing like Brooke. Brooke was a bottle blonde with an asymmetrical bob who wore lots of makeup. His Noëlle would be natural. She'd have wavy, black hair, and her lashes would be thick and real. Brooke was as tall as he was, five-eleven. His Noëlle would be so small he could rest his chin on her head when he embraced her.

Of course there were things about Brooke he would want in his Noëlle. Brooke was bright. His Noëlle would be brilliant. Brooke was athletic, although workouts had to fit her schedule. His Noëlle would be fit, but also delicate and graceful, and she would love to go on his long spur-of-the-moment walks. Brooke had an angular, boyish figure. His Noëlle would be slender, but shapely with feminine hips and high, round breasts. That was important. He didn't want her to be built like a guy.

And she'd like to eat. Brooke spent her days around anorexic models, and she avoided food like it was poison. She was a talented designer, though, and David wanted his Noëlle to be great at something too. In the book she was a healer, but his dream was of a modern woman. He'd figure it out later. For the moment, he was content to fall asleep imagining his lovely Noëlle who would be happy just to be with him.

David woke refreshed at noon. This was the longest he'd slept since the break-up. He made coffee, grabbed the leftover duck with noodles out of the fridge and went to his drawing board to sketch. He made thumbnails of several concepts for his cover, chose the best three and drew them in more detail. But not having internet made it difficult to research costumes.

David dialed Pascal. He'd made the original call to get the internet hooked up; maybe he could help. "Hey buddy, I'm still not connected, and I need it for work. Can you call and see what's up?"

"You know it takes a few weeks in France."

"I know but..."

"Hold on." Pascal spoke to someone in French.

Shit, David thought. He didn't have time for this.

"I'm at work," said Pascal when he came back on. "I'll get to it as soon as I can. Give me the number again."

David would just have to wing the clothing based on past research, scan the sketches and submit them from a cybercafé.

On his way out, in the late afternoon, he noticed a piece of paper wedged in his mailbox. His heart did a drumroll as he read, "David, I left a package with your landlord. Hope you're doing well. Brooke."

David went to the Hamidous' door and knocked. No answer. He knocked harder. Damn. They weren't home. The closest cybercafé was in the twelfth. He couldn't wait. It was getting late, and he had to email those scans.

When he knocked again two hours later, Madame Hamidou answered. She left him waiting long enough for his mood to swing from anxious desire to get Brooke's package, to annoyance, to anger. She finally reappeared with two boxes: the one from Brooke and another filled with baklava.

"For me?" asked David. Now he felt ashamed for his impatience. God, he was a jerk.

Madame Hamidou smiled and said something in French.

David wasn't sure if he should try one on the spot, but Madame was watching expectantly so he tasted one of the sticky diamond-shaped pastries. It was chewy-sweet and buttery, with a hint of salt from the pistachios, and had a surprising aftertaste of roses.

"Mmm," he said making a show of how delicious they were. He ate another. This delighted Madame Hamidou, and she started speaking rapidly, pointing at the box then at David. He wondered how he would ever get upstairs. Finally he put his hands up in an attempt to pantomime, "I don't understand." She seemed to get that and let him go.

He sprinted up the two flights, fumbled with the door lock, hurried to the futon and tore open Brooke's package. The baklava turned to lead in his stomach. Inside were a small green velvet box and an envelope. David knew that velvet box. It was her engagement ring. He opened the envelope hoping it contained some sort of explanation, the kind that said it's not your fault, I'm just going through something, but give me time, and I'll get over it. Instead it was a bill for two weeks rent and electricity.

David pressed his palms hard against his eyes and rocked forward, breathing through clenched teeth. He wasn't thinking about Brooke at all. He was thinking of his father, hating him because he had been right.

ॐॐ

The next few weeks passed in a blur of frustration. David tried calling Brooke a couple more times. The second time he waited through her incomprehensible message and said, "Hey Brooke, just wanted to touch base. Things are going great. I'd love to show you my new apartment..." BEEP. He was cut off.

He dulled his loneliness and anger with work, but the fact that he still didn't have internet was torture. Finally Pascal called to tell him it was hooked up and to give him the code. David was so delighted he invited the guys over to celebrate.

"Thanks again for calling the provider for me," David said after dinner. "You want Calvados or Vermouth?"

"Vermouth. *Merci.*" Pascal took a sip. "You know, you should have had service three weeks ago. Have you looked into taking French classes, yet, *mon cher*?"

"Not yet," said David. "But even if I were taking classes, I would never have been able to deal with this."

"You would if you had started lessons when you first moved to Paris. If you're going to live here, learn the language."

David felt his temper begin to rise. "I've been swamped, and having to constantly use cybercafés hasn't made things any easier."

"I'm busy, too, and having to make calls for you doesn't make my life any easier."

"It's great you have so much work, David," Dan interjected looking at the painting of Noëlle. "This is wonderful."

"Thanks, Dan." David didn't need Pascal's shit right now. "It's the cover art for Lilia Dufort's new book."

"You captured something in the girl's eyes, a certain pathos but also an intensity. She's beautiful. Who is she?"

"I made her up. Borrowed the pose from Delacroix."

"Is this you behind her?" asked Pascal.

"Yup." Now David was embarrassed. "Me as the young duke with a slightly straighter nose."

"I think you make a very handsome duke." David took this as Pascal's way of apologizing. "You should let your hair grow."

"I'll consider it."

It had been a while since David had seen his friends, and despite Pascal's harping, he hadn't wanted the evening to end. Their presence made the silence after they left more profound. For a couple of weeks David had depended on Noëlle to keep him company while he painted her, but now that the illustration was finished he had to mail it to the publisher.

"I'll miss you," he said to the painting. "And you probably won't be back for months."

She looked at him as she always did, with longing.

The next morning he carefully packed the illustration and crept down the stairs to the courtyard. He had to get out without the Hamidous spotting him. The weeks of going to cybercafés had taught him that if he let his landlords start talking they wouldn't stop, and he'd have a hell of a time escaping. It would have been bad enough if he understood what they were saying, but he didn't, and their chattiness had become exasperating.

Sure enough, Monsieur Hamidou was there tending his herb pots. Just ignore him, David thought, and he hurried out to the street without acknowledging his loquacious landlord. When he returned an hour later Monsieur Hamidou was still there, but he turned his back and walked inside without a word. Over the next couple of days David hardly saw the Hamidous, and when he did, they shunned him. What had he done to make them dislike him all of a sudden? It hurt. Now that they didn't want to speak with him, David missed their baffling chatter. Well, screw it. At least he could come and go as he pleased.

Not that he wanted to go out much. If it wasn't full out raining, the hostile Parisian sky seemed to spit cold drizzle at him whenever he left his apartment. And no matter what he did, he couldn't warm up. He got up to stretch and put on a sweatshirt one afternoon when his cell phone rang.

"For cripes sake, I'm working," he grumbled. Then he looked at the phone. It was his art director from Pantaloon.

"Hello?"

"Hallo, David!" said a deep British voice. "It's Rich Black. Listen, that cover you did for *Foxglove and Foolscap* is absolutely sterling."

"Thanks, Rich."

"Everyone here is just arse over tit for it... And so is Lilia."

"She's seen the final?"

"She has. Actually that's why I'm calling. She wants to meet you." A long pause. "David? You still there?"

"I'm here. I don't meet the authors, Rich."

"I know, and we usually discourage it, but you know

she lives in Paris."

"No, I didn't know that."

"Listen, David, she's an important author for us."

"I know." David sighed. "When does she want to meet?"

"Don't know. I'd like to give her your number if that's all right?"

Lilia called the next day. When she told him she lived in Passy, he suggested they meet somewhere in the sixteenth; it would give him the opportunity to visit his old neighborhood.

"How funny that you lived here, and we never met," she said.

David was meeting Lilia at La Coïncidence. He intentionally arrived early and went by Brooke's apartment. He felt like a fool standing there staring up at her window. Had he really hoped to see her? That was unlikely at lunchtime on a weekday. And if he did see her, what would he say? *Gee Brooke, I was on my way to the lunch from hell, and I thought I'd walk several blocks out of my way just to annoy myself further by bumping into you.*

Just then a cloud passed overhead casting a dark shadow over the flat façade of Brooke's building. It seemed to say, "You're no longer welcome here." Well fine. He had never liked the charmless building, anyway. It was new and lacked the elegance of its Haussmannian neighbors. He raised his collar, crossed the street, and headed toward the Rue Mesnil and his meeting with Lilia.

The first thing David thought upon seeing her was, *she's so tiny.* He had imagined the author of such sappy romances would be an overweight, middle-aged woman with frumpy blue hair. But Lilia was pretty for a woman her age. She was about five feet tall and slender with straight salt and pepper hair cut in a pageboy, hazel eyes slightly magnified by silver-rimmed glasses, and bubble-gum pink lipstick.

"I'm delighted to finally meet you," she said shaking his hand. "Please don't worry, I won't try to tell you your business. I know why they like to keep us authors away from the illustrators, but Richard Black told me you lived in Paris, and I just had to thank you in person."

David was surprised at how comfortable he felt with her. He was usually reserved, but Lilia was so kind and engaging, he fell into conversation with her as if they'd been friends for years.

"You know, I've loved all your cover art, but that last painting," she paused to sip her wine. "How did you do it?"

"Well, I usually work in acrylic on canvas paper so the illustrations are easier to scan. And, for your books I do a fair amount of research to get the costumes and settings right."

"Yes, but you managed to capture Noëlle as if you knew her."

"You described her very well. To tell the truth, *Foxglove and Foolscap* was my favorite of your books."

"Mine, too. It was more historical novel and less gummy romance, wasn't it?"

"Well, yeah. I'm sorry. I'm not into the sappy stuff."

"I've done quite well with that formula, but I was bored. I missed good old-fashioned research. Did you know when I first came to Paris I was an art historian?"

As the conversation progressed David learned that Lilia had lived in Paris for thirty years, that she had a daughter, and that she was widowed.

"And you never remarried?"

"No. My husband was the love of my life. His loss shattered me. I wrote the story of our romance as a means of working through my grief. Gradually, I invented other stories and was surprised when they started selling. When my daughter was in school, the novels kept me company."

"I understand. The painting of Noëlle kept me company too. I got the assignment right after my fiancée broke up with me."

There was something about this warm little woman that made David want to tell her the story of his split with Brooke.

"And you think she left because you couldn't speak French?" Lilia asked when he had finished.

"That's part of it. I made her handle everything, and she got tired of it. And it bugged her to have to translate for me all the time."

"Hmmm. Are you planning to stay in Paris?"

"I have to."

"Because your work is here?"

"Because if I go back I'll never hear the end of it from my father." David took a bite of his cheeseburger and wondered again why he was telling this to a stranger. But Lilia sat watching him intently, and he felt compelled to go on. "My father is all about success. He's a well-known architect who holds himself and everyone else to a very high standard. He told me I couldn't hack it in a foreign country. He doesn't think I can hack most things. If I go back it means admitting to him that he was right, that I failed again."

"Is your father Samuel Glaser?"

"You know him?"

"I know of him. I know he has a reputation as a perfectionist."

"That's one way to put it."

"So you want to stay in Paris just to prove to your father that you can? Do you even like Paris?"

"To be honest, I don't know. I mean it's beautiful, but I feel so disconnected, like I don't belong."

"How so?"

"I never know what's going on around me. I can't communicate with people I need to like my landlord or my internet provider. It's like I live in Paris, but I'm not part of it."

Lilia rested her chin on her hand and looked at David for a long time. "I guess the obvious question is why don't you learn to speak French?"

He looked at his plate.

"David, are you afraid to try to learn French? No, hear me out. I know I'm being forward, but sometimes when we have a very critical parent we become afraid of trying."

David shrugged, but he felt comforted when she smiled and reached across the table to touch his arm.

"I'm speaking from experience," she went on. "I did the same thing to my daughter."

"You don't strike me as the type to criticize."

"Oh, I do it out of love. I always think I know what will make her happy better than she does."

"Does she agree?"

"Of course not. And now, because I pushed so hard, she is immediately against anything I say."

"I doubt my father does it out of love, but you're probably right. Thanks to his constant tirades I'm terrified of failure." He couldn't believe he was admitting this, but added, "The truth is I'm afraid I won't be able to learn French. I was terrible at Spanish in high school."

"There you go," she said. "Listen, I know a great school. It's very relaxed, and you can progress at your own pace. I really think you should try it if you're going to stay in Paris, and I hope you do stay because I'd like us to be friends."

David laughed when she told him the name of the school. "That's the same one my buddy Dan recommended back in September. Maybe it's a sign." He grinned mischievously. "Or maybe you think you know what's best for me too."

That made her laugh. "I probably do!"

By the time he and Lilia said goodbye it was nearly five o'clock. They agreed to meet again soon, and David headed for the Trocadéro Métro. He was in such a good mood even the rush hour crowd shoving on the stairs didn't bother him.

When the train arrived, an old woman was struggling to make her way to the front of the throng. David used his body to block the people behind him so she could board safely. He stepped onto the car behind her and looked up just in time to see Brooke pushing her way off.

Shoulder to shoulder, Brooke looked directly at him then allowed her face to go blank and looked away. She wasn't alone. As the doors of the car closed, he watched through the glass as a tall blond man put his arm around her and led her away.

David felt queasy. He swayed and held the pole tightly. The old woman he helped onto the train pulled on his jacket and said something he didn't understand. She frowned when someone else took the seat beside her. David shrugged and continued staring numbly through the glass of the train doors. He didn't move when they opened, and passengers pushed past him. He didn't care if he was in the way. He just held on tight as the train rocked, and the people behind smashed him against the doors. When he got out at busy Châtelet, he couldn't remember which way to go, so he leaned against the tile wall and closed his eyes to get his bearings.

He hadn't seen or spoken to Brooke in two months. During that time he had often fantasized about her running into him. She would pass him on the street when he was hurrying some place important. He'd give her a casual peck on the cheek, then rush off without a care. She would see him in a restaurant, and he would excuse himself from his table full of laughing friends to say a quick hello. Or his favorite, she would see him with another woman, his Noëlle, with whom he would be speaking French. In that one he wouldn't even notice her, but she'd see his Noëlle laugh and kiss him. Brooke had actually seen him today, though. She had looked right at him and pretended he didn't exist.

It was full dark by the time he got home. He could see lights on in the Hamidous' apartment and in several of the windows on the upper two floors. He hated coming home to an empty apartment. He hated cooking for himself, but the thought of eating alone in a restaurant, or just grabbing take-out, depressed him more. He didn't even bother to turn on the lights, just kicked his shoes off and flopped down on his futon. He shifted to pull his cell phone out of his pocket and noticed he had a voicemail.

"Hello, David, it's Lilia. I just wanted to tell you again what a wonderful time I had meeting you today. Also, I took the liberty of getting the number of that school for you. Please don't think I'm pushy. Just consider me enthusiastic."

David was nervous about calling the next morning.

"Hello?" he said to the receptionist's *bonjour*.

"Hello," she replied in English, and he slouched in relief. "Yes, we will have a beginner's class starting the first week of November that will last for six weeks."

David thought the two-hour-a-day schedule she described sounded a lot more intense than either Dan or Lilia had led him to believe, but so close to the holidays his work had slowed, and he had nothing better to do from two to four.

༄༅

"*Bonjour, tout le monde*," said the instructor. She wrote

her name, Madame Petit, on the whiteboard in large block letters. She continued speaking in French, using her hands and some silly drawings to aid her students' comprehension, making it clear that only French would be spoken. *Oh shit*, David thought.

By the end of the first ten minutes, he learned he was the only American in a class of six Chinese exchange students, two Polish women, a guy from Argentina and an Iranian man. At least the class was for true beginners: Madame Petit began with how to say hello.

"*Bonjour*," she said to each student, extending a chubby hand to shake.

After everyone had greeted her and each other, Madame Petit drew a crude building with a sign over the door that said, *Le Magasin*. Then she reached into a canvas bag beside her desk and pulled out some fake fruit, a couple of empty cookie boxes and a roll of toilet paper. That got a laugh.

"*Le magasin*," she said and waved her arms for the class to repeat. She made some more drawings: a hat, a dress, a bird-like thing, a bottle. She pointed to her building, picked up her purse and pantomimed buying the objects. David understood. *Un magasin* was a store.

"Monsieur Glaser," said Madame Petit, motioning him to approach.

She signaled that he was to come into the store and pretended she was the clerk. David came in, picked up a plastic banana and held it out to her. "*Non, non*," she said, and led him back to the "door," a space between two desks. Then she sat again with her hands folded and her eyebrows raised.

David looked at her. What the hell was he supposed to do?

"Ah," said Madame Petit. She gestured for him to sit in the chair then entered the "door" herself by squeezing through the gap between the desks. "*Bonjour* Monsieur!"

she sang at him.

"*Bonjour*, Madame," said David.

"*Très bien!*" she said. David realized he had done something right, but what?

Madame went through the same pantomime with a few of the other students until they and David understood that they were to greet her when they entered the store and say good-bye when they left.

The next day Madame Petit blocked the doorway to the classroom with her ample body so no one could enter. David and his classmates stared at her dumbly until one of the Chinese students said, "*Bonjour*, Madame."

"*Bonjour*, Mademoiselle!" said Madame Petit. She stepped aside and allowed the young woman to pass, but blocked the door again until each student had greeted her properly.

David wished he had been the one to realize what to do. In the past he had noticed French people always greeted each other, but he thought it was because they were acquainted. Now it dawned on him: It wasn't that the people knew each other; the French expected to be greeted whenever you encountered them.

ஒ௸

"So you just walked past him?" said Pascal.

David sipped wine while Dan and Pascal prepared omelets and salad. "I was in a hurry. When the Hamidous start talking, I can't get away."

"And she gave you baklava?"

"Yeah, once."

"Have you ever done anything nice for her?"

"I let her talk at me."

"You just said you don't." Pascal shook his head. "This is why we say you Americans are rude."

"Pascal, don't be so hard on him."

"Daniel, he's lived here for five years, and he's just learning this?"

"Christ, Pascal, at least I'm finally learning."

"Too bad you didn't learn sooner. You might not have lost Brooke." David saw Dan shoot a warning glance at Pascal. "No," he said. "He need to understand this." When Pascal got upset his English degraded.

"You saw Brooke?" said David.

"I have lunch with her last week."

David crossed his arms challenging him to go on.

"Pascal, this isn't a conversation we need to have," said Dan as he handed David an omelet. "So how are your classes going?"

"Great. I can actually speak a little now." He glared at Pascal. "And I understand a lot more."

"You treat Brooke same as your landlord," Pascal said. "You ignore her needs. All you think is what you need, how you feel."

"Is that what she told you?"

"Yes, but I see this myself. You want other people, your friends, to do for you. If they cannot, you become angry. You are angry with me when I cannot call the internet provider for you right away."

"No I wasn't."

"You were. I could tell. You don't call us for three weeks until I finally fix it for you."

"I didn't want to bother you, and I couldn't call myself because I couldn't speak French."

"You think you're the only American in Paris? They have English speakers there. You just like to feel sad for yourself."

David felt his face growing hot. "Jeezus, is that what Brooke told you?"

"She say she ask you many times to learn French, but you like not understanding. It force her to take care of you. She say you force someone to take care of you so you feel loved. Then you embarrass her when she try to make good connections with colleagues because you cannot understand. She say if something is not easy for you, you walk away. You can't give to others, but you take very well."

"Fuck you, Pascal."

Dan stood up and put his hand firmly on Pascal's shoulder. "*Arrête!*" David had never heard Dan raise his voice, but at least he understood the word "stop."

"You know, David, other people can be having troubles that are not about you." Pascal was sobbing. Dan put his arm around him and led him to the bedroom. It was all too weird.

"I'm so sorry," Dan said when he came back.

"What the hell is going on? What have I done that's so wrong?"

"He's very upset tonight. Here, have some more wine." Dan divided the rest of the bottle between their two glasses. The omelets sat untasted before them.

"Did I insult him that badly?"

"Of course not. His mother called. His dad has stage four lung cancer."

"Oh shit."

"Pascal told her he'd come down for Christmas, and she said his father doesn't want to see him. He considers him an abomination."

"She actually said that?"

"Unbelievable, right?" said Dan. "I'm taking Pascal to Nîmes for Christmas. We've got friends down there."

"How long will you be gone?" David felt his chest tighten. What would he do for the holidays with them gone?

"We'll go down on the twentieth and come back on January third."

David downed the last of his wine and stood to go.

"You haven't eaten," said Dan.

"It's OK. Go take care of Pascal. He needs you."

A flutist was playing The Dance of the Reed Pipes from The Nutcracker in the Hôtel de Ville Métro station. Normally David would have passed by, wallowing in his hurt feelings, but this time he stopped to listen. How could anyone make a living like that, he wondered, and tossed a couple euros into the open flute case before walking to his platform in time to the music.

The two-beat rhythm of the Tchaikovsky piece was still stuck in his head when he got off the Métro. Belleville twinkled with Christmas lights, every one matching the beat of the music. It seemed each flickering tree and blinking balcony was saying, "On-off. A-lone. So-sad."

Why did the prospect of spending the holidays alone bother him so much? He was Jewish. He'd never celebrated Christmas growing up. Heck, his family never really celebrated Hanukkah; they went out for Chinese on one of the nights. He could do that. But he'd still be alone. Maybe he'd get a television. He was starting to understand more French. He'd need the practice. But he only had one more class.

A-lone. One-class. Too-bad.

David got to class early the next afternoon with a big plate of chocolate chip cookies for the Christmas party.

"*Salut*," said Juan Diego, the Argentinian, coming up behind him. He and David had gotten coffee together a few times after class and could communicate fairly well between their high school Spanish and English and their broken French.

Gradually the other students assembled in the hall outside the locked classroom.

"Where teacher?" said one of the Chinese girls.

"Do we..." the Polish woman paused, thinking. "Do we hear?" she tried.

"We wait," said David, understanding she had mixed up the verbs for "to hear" and "to wait."

"*Pardon,*" said a real French voice from behind the milling students. "*Excusez-moi.*"

A small, dark haired woman pushed to the door and unlocked it.

After all the students had greeted her and taken their seats she explained in simple French, "Madame Petit is very sorry. She is ill and cannot come to the last class. My name is Jeanne Burghelle. I am a teacher in the next level. I will teach your final class today."

David sat mute and paralyzed staring at her wide-eyed.

"*Ça va, Monsieur?*" she asked.

"*Oui,*" he whispered.

"*Pardon?*"

"*Oui,*" he said a little louder.

Some of the other students giggled. Juan Diego gave David a playful slap on the back that seemed to say, *Yeah, she's a far cry from Madame Petit.*

Mademoiselle Burghelle smiled at him.

The class passed in a blur. One minute they were going over reflexive verbs, the next they were eating sweets from their various countries and wishing each other a joyful Christmas. The whole time David gave himself psychic pinches: He blinked, rubbed his eyes, turned away, then back. Is this real? This can't be real. My God, she's real.

She was his painting, his Noëlle, come to life: the large, intense gray eyes with thick dark lashes, long wavy black hair and full pink lips. She was obviously slender, though it was difficult to discern her figure under her heavy black sweater. But she wore leggings and boots that accentuated shapely legs. David looked up quickly when she approached to sample one of his cookies. He noticed she had green and blue stains around her cuticles and under her short nails. Aha!

"You are an artist?" he asked.

"How did you know?"

"Your..." He didn't know the word so he pointed to his own fingernails.

"Ah, yes. Disgusting. I cannot clean them." She laughed. Her laugh was beautiful. She was beautiful.

He was staring at her again. She started to turn away so he said, "Me, too."

"What?"

"I'm a painter. I do acrylics. And you?"

"I paint in oils. You understand?"

"Yes."

Then she turned to speak with the Iranian man. Damn. How could he get her attention again?

When class ended, David took his time covering his plate of cookies with plastic wrap. There had been so many sweets at the party the plate was still piled high.

"You want go café?" Juan Diego asked.

"I cannot. I send you text, yes?" David tilted his head subtly toward Jeanne.

"Oh ho!" Juan Diego winked and left.

Jeanne put her coat on and looked at David. He couldn't read her expression.

"I must lock the door," she said.

"Do you drink coffee with me?" he blurted.

She paused before answering, which he hoped was a good sign. He held his breath.

"I cannot," she finally said. "It is forbidden to—a word he didn't understand—with students."

"*Fréquenter*?" he asked.

"Socialize," she said in perfect English.

He felt his face start to crumble. He couldn't lose her.

"But I'm not really your student."

"I cannot."

Cannot or will not? David watched his dream stride briskly away. He slumped against the wall beside the locked classroom door. His throat squeezed shut. When he was finally able to move again he trudged like a condemned man out of the building toward the Métro.

Christ, did every Métro station in Paris have buskers playing cloying Christmas music? David waited for his train at Opéra with his free hand covering his right ear, the one closest to the musicians. In his left he held the plate of cookies. Someone tapped him on the shoulder, and he nearly dumped them on the platform.

"I'm sorry. I didn't mean to startle you." It was Jeanne Burghelle.

"What are you doing here?"

"I'm on my way home."

"Where's that?"

"I live in Belleville."

"So do I."

She stood beside him on the crowded train. They came out onto the street across from La Veilleuse.

Jeanne said, "Perhaps I'll get a coffee, and you'll just happen to get one too."

As they sipped their coffees, David asked, "Why did you change your mind?"

"Well, you looked so hurt when I refused you after class. But also, I was curious. It's too coincidental that we're both artists, we both live in Belleville, and I bumped into you again at Opéra."

"You're superstitious?"

"A little. I like signs."

"Then have I got a sign for you."

"What do you mean?"

"I've painted you."

She laughed. "What?"

David told her about his illustration, but when he

finished she had a funny look on her face.

"David, what's your last name?"

"Glaser, why?"

"I know your work. You're very good."

"Thanks. I'd love to see yours sometime."

She didn't respond. Had he said something wrong? She looked at her watch. "I have to get going."

"I'll walk you home."

"No, that's OK." She stood and put on her coat. "Thanks again for the coffee. It was nice to meet you."

"Wait a minute. That's it?"

She held out her hand to shake.

"Can I see you again?"

"I don't think so," she said.

David grabbed his coat and the plate of cookies and hurried after her, but she had disappeared by the time he got out the door.

He wanted to tear down every tinsel decoration strung across every street and cut the wires to all the damned lights. He hated every smiling person heading with a friend or lover into the overfilled cafés. He detested the blow-up Santas and the fake snow. Most of all he loathed himself. How could he screw that up so badly? His father was right, damn it. He was a total fuck-up.

But what did he do wrong? Maybe she thought the story of his illustration was kinky. Shit. Why did he tell her? She probably thought he was some kind of psycho. And at the moment his emotions were so out of control he felt like one. At least he knew her name, and he knew she lived somewhere near him because she got out at the same stop. But if he tried to find her she might think he was a stalker. He could sign up for another class. She said she taught the next level. He would request her.

Having a plan did little to lighten his foul mood. To make things worse, the automatic light didn't come on in

the courtyard of his building. Some illumination came
from the Hamidous' apartment, but the stairs were black.
David stumbled on the first step and slammed his shin
and elbow trying to save his cookies.

"God damn it," he shouted rearranging them on the
plate. He'd tell that Hamidou a thing or two. He knew
the word for light and how to say no.

David pounded on their door. Madame Hamidou
parted the curtain and peered out at him. The expression
on her face disturbed him. My God, she's afraid of me,
he realized. Fear always brought his father to mind. He
thought of how terrified he always felt before the old
man let loose on him. Madame Hamidou probably
thought he was going to yell at her. And he was, wasn't
he?

Monsieur Hamidou opened the door. He wasn't
smiling.

Before he realized what he was doing, David held out
the plate of chocolate chip cookies and said, "For you."
When Monsieur Hamidou just stared at him he went on,
"I am sorry to be bad. I do not understand, but now I
learn French. I learn to say hello. I learn that this is
important. I give you this to be friend if you please."

Madame Hamidou squeezed in front of her husband.
A huge smile brightened her round face. She accepted
the plate and gently led David into the apartment by the
arm. She stopped in the entry and gestured to a rack of
shoes. David took his off and put them neatly beside the
others.

"Monsieur Glaser, please sit down." She directed him
to sit on a couch then took an armchair opposite a low
coffee table. Monsieur Hamidou had followed them in
but went through to the kitchen. David could hear him
rattling pots.

Madame Hamidou said something David didn't
understand.

"Slowly, please," he said.

"How—did—you—learn—to—speak—French?"

David told her about his class and did his best to answer her questions about himself. Monsieur Hamidou returned with a teapot on a tray and three glasses. Then he gracefully poured each glass from a surprising height.

David took a sip. It was sweet and minty. Monsieur Hamidou refilled their glasses as soon as they were empty.

"The first glass is as gentle as life, the second is as strong as love, and the third is as bitter as death," he explained.

Their conversation wasn't easy. David used his cell phone to look up vocabulary he didn't know or words the Hamidous used that he didn't understand, but it was fun. They ate cookies and laughed and muddled through stories of who they were and why they were in Paris. David finally understood that the Hamidous weren't French, either. Why hadn't he realized this?

He left their apartment two hours later with a feeling of connection that warmed him. He had friends, his own friends that he made himself. Of course he had Pascal and Dan, and he supposed he was friends with Lilia, although he hadn't seen her since October. Then there was Juan Diego from class, and now the Hamidous. He wished he could have been friends with Jeanne Burghelle. More than anything, he wanted to get to know her.

He got out his sketchbook and drew her sipping coffee at La Veilleuse. He drew her again from a different angle, and again. He got up and went to his computer to look at the scan of his painting of Noëlle to compare it to his sketches. An email from Lilia popped up.

"Hello, David! I'm having a small dinner party next Saturday night, and I'd love you to come. I'm killing two birds with one stone. It's a Christmas party, but I'm also celebrating the publication of *Foxglove and Foolscap*. Please say you'll join us. Lilia."

David wrote back immediately, "Thanks Lilia, I'd love to. Just tell me when and where, and what I can bring. David."

※

Lilia said not to bring anything "but himself," but he hadn't wanted to arrive empty-handed. He thought about the joy on the Hamidous' faces when he gave them the plate of chocolate chip cookies. It still made him smile. Brooke usually brought wine or flowers to the parties they attended. Lilia would probably like flowers, he thought.

"Oh David, is that you behind there?" Lilia said when she opened the door.

"It's me." He was holding the biggest Christmas plant they had at the florist.

"My dear, this is the most beautiful poinsettia I've ever seen. We'll use it for a centerpiece."

"It's heavy, I'll carry it for you," he said, shrugging out of his jacket.

David looked around as he followed Lilia into her apartment. It had magnificent high ceilings and enormous windows, but best of all, her art collection was phenomenal. Several handsome paintings adorned the walls, many clearly by the same artist. Guests gathered around a low marble table that held an elaborate plate of crudité. Some stood and others sat on an elegant couch and chairs. David could hear music from The Nutcracker playing softly under the murmur of their voices.

"Lilia, this place is beautiful," he said. "I love your paintings."

She got a twinkle in her eye. "Would you like to meet the artist?"

"He's here?"

"Follow me." She led him to an ornate Christmas tree where two women stood chatting with an older man. She gently tapped the smaller woman's shoulder.

"David, I'd like you to meet my daughter, Jeanne Noëlle Burghelle."

Jeanne Noëlle looked from him to her mother and back again. David had seen that wide-eyed stare before. At least this time she couldn't run.

"*Chérie*, this is my illustrator, David Glaser," Lilia went on gayly. "I told Noëlle all about you, David. I wanted to get you two together sooner, but my daughter is very elusive." She winked at him.

Lilia also introduced David to the taller woman and the man, but all he heard was the Dance of the Reed Pipes playing in the background. This time, the rhythm of the music didn't match the blinking of the lights on the tree.

"Oh for heaven's sake, David," Lilia was saying, "give me that plant. John, would you carry this to the table for me, dear? What do you think, Audrey, is it too big for a centerpiece? Noëlle, get David some champagne, will you?"

They stood staring at each other.

"Champagne?" she finally said.

"Please."

He followed her to a table where bottles and champagne flutes were arranged around dishes of hors d'oeuvres. A large painting hung above the table. It was a nude in motion. The solid parts of the figure were interspersed with fluid lines. The colors were rich and unexpected, but the effect was as if the heavy impasto was as much actual skin as paint.

"This is beautiful," he said. "Is it yours?"

She handed him a glass. "Yes."

He wanted to tell her she was beautiful, too, but he didn't dare. She wore black again, but this time it was a short, clingy dress with a simple boat neck in front that plunged in back. Whatever questions he had about her real figure compared with the one he had envisioned were clearly answered.

"Why do you stare at me that way?" she asked. "It's creepy."

"Oh God, I'm sorry. It's just that I imagined you for so long. I guess I'm just surprised at how accurate I was."

"That's disgusting."

"Why?"

"You don't even know me. I don't want you or anyone else thinking of me that way."

"What way?"

"You don't get it, do you? My mother described me so precisely that you were able to paint me as if you knew me. Now my face, and most of my breasts I might add, are plastered all over her novel which is piled in bookshop windows all over the world." She groaned. "She even gave the character my name."

"You go by Jeanne," he said stupidly.

"But most people know me as Jeanne Noëlle."

"And Burghelle?"

"That was my father's name."

"Not Dufort?"

Jeanne Noëlle laughed. "*Maman* didn't tell you? No, of course she wouldn't."

"Tell me what?"

"Lilia Dufort is a pseudonym."

"I should have guessed. A lot of writers use pseudonyms."

"She says she needs to protect her privacy. Unfortunately, she doesn't see anything wrong with exposing me to the world."

David looked across the room at Lilia. She was smiling warmly as she bustled among her guests pouring champagne. To him she seemed the essence of kindness and love. "But she made you her heroine," he said.

"Some heroine." Jeanne Noëlle took a sip of champagne and coughed when it went down the wrong way. "She nearly burned me at the stake! I love my mother, I really do, but she's a busybody who has no respect for other people's boundaries. Don't think she didn't tell me all about you."

"What did she tell you?"

"That your famous father is abusive, and you want to stay in Paris to be as far away from him as possible. And, your fiancée dumped you because you couldn't speak French..."

"That's a pretty flat portrait," he interrupted.

"I'm sorry. I've said too much."

"No, actually you haven't said enough. And your mother probably didn't either. The truth is my fiancée dumped me, as you say, because I'm too much like my father. I'm impatient, self-centered and terrified of failure. I was more concerned with my own needs than hers. I'm afraid I did the same thing to you. To me you were a wonderful character in a book. Then I made you into a painting, and I fell in love with the image I created. But that wasn't you. I'd like to get to know the real you, if you're willing, and I'd like you to learn first-hand about me."

Lilia called, "*A table*, everyone. Dinner is served!"

Jeanne Noëlle looked up at him. David knew that expression. It was the one he had painted. Then she smiled, put her arm through his, and led him to the table.

Joyful Noise

Laura Schalk

My girlfriend, Mina, is a confirmed shower-singer, making up little two-verse songs that she warbles in a loop during her ablutions. I usually find this quite sexy, and it's often the cue for me to shed whatever I'm wearing and join her in the shower for some soapy fooling around.

"I heard a ruuuumor / That you haaaave a tumor… "

But Christmas Eve morning, when her warm alto wafted out of the guest bathroom into the lemon-hued kitchen where my brother, James, his live-in girlfriend, Pamela, and I were having breakfast, my penis jumped to attention then beat a quick retreat. I was infinitely more embarrassed than turned on. The bright smile fixed on Pamela's face did not waver, however. I could tell she was the kind of woman who would neither acknowledge nor comment on any noise emanating from a bathroom.

James was totally engrossed in Barron's, and since he's deaf when he's reading intently, I hoped Mina's singing would bypass him entirely.

"This is great coffee, Pamela." I couldn't decide

whether 'Sunshine Pammie' or 'Perky Pam' was going to be my nickname for her.

"Thank you Christian—or do you prefer Chris? It's organic Fair Trade coffee. Finally we get the good stuff out here in the boonies! Would you like another muffin?"

"People usually call me Chris," I said. That fucker James, he probably told Pamela my middle name too, and she'll be hailing Christian Xavier the next time brotherly love forces me to disembark at the East Norwalk train station. No one's called me Christian in years; even my dead grandmother and my fifth grade teacher knew better. "And I'm OK for the moment, but the muffins were delicious. Are they homemade?" Actually they were dry, and I could see a Waldbaum's in-store bakery plastic muffin coffin on top of the recycle bin.

I kept going before Pamela could either lie or own up to buying baked goods at the supermarket. I was going to take control of this situation, goddammit. "You guys have totally made this place your own. It's hard to believe you've only lived here a few months. The kitchen is really airy and bright... but I bet that's your touch as opposed to James'." This cued conspiratorial chuckles on both our parts, and I had given her an excuse to gaze lovingly at my dark-haired, square-jawed banker brother who wouldn't know a window treatment if it leapt off the shelf at Ikea and tried to strangle him.

"Oh thank you, Chris!" She sounded genuinely moved. "We're only renting so it's not worth putting a huge amount of effort and expense into this place, but I think the kitchen is the most important room in any home so I did repaint the walls, and those are our own curtains. Can you believe I had to go to battle with the rental agency to get the landlord to put in a proper stove with an oven? As if we could make do with just a microwave!" She clacked her coffee cup on the table, and I thought the light of battle was going to flare again, but

James turned a crackling page, and Pamela gave a little snort and continued in a milder tone. "I also chose that sea green for the guest bedroom. It was such a horrible dark brown before. You would have had nightmares sleeping there."

Pamela enumerated the various improvements she would make, were she an owner and not a tenant of the single-family, three-bedroom colonial at 12 Gregory Boulevard: Mediterranean blue tiles in her and James' bathroom; a nasturtium theme in the dining room; a proper laundry room in the basement. She then segued to some of the advantages of living there: the easy driving commute for both of them, proximity to her parents, and the amazing coincidence that her childhood pastor from Westport had taken semi-retirement at St. Matthew's Episcopal Church, which was practically walking distance from the house.

Pamela was telling me about the really exceptionally talented carol singers at St. Matthew's Midnight Mass as Mina added syncopation to her ditty: "I heard [beat] a rumor [beat] that you've got [beat] a tu-mor."

My brother dropped his paper and shot me a look that said, *Your girlfriend is fucking weird.*

I shot him one back: *Your girlfriend is wearing a flowered apron, she just handed you a cup of coffee in a Garfield mug, and she's dragging your ass to church tonight.*

I had more to say and tried to really focus my eyes, to deliver a laser-look capable of carrying all my meaning to James: *Once Pamela clinches the deal and you're married, you'll be leading God-fearing Cub Scout troops on weekend retreats in Lyme Disease State Park. And you're going to have a millstone mortgage around your neck and be eating, sleeping and fucking in pastel hell for the rest of your natural life.*

James smiled, stretched his arms over his head till the joints popped and said, "Hey Pam, what's the program for today?"

"Well, I thought Chris and Mina might like to take a walk and explore our neck of the woods. Then we'll go out for a quick bite of lunch, pick up the roast on the way back and start getting dinner ready. Drinks are at seven, and we'll eat at seven-thirty. I had thought to have champagne and decorate the tree as a group once my parents got here, but I just couldn't wait…"

We had arrived after eleven the night before and been given a somewhat perfunctory tour of the house—but I had noted a stunted conifer in one corner of the living room, ensnared in silver tinsel.

"Awesome shower. You guys have great water pressure." Mina had twisted her wet hair into a bun and secured it with a chopstick. She was wearing skinny jeans and one of my turtlenecks, and looked fresh but sleepy still.

"Here babe, let me get you some coffee." I tipped half the pot into an oversized mug bearing a rubicund Santa face and a couple of leering elves, and added a slug of milk. "Pamela was just giving us our marching orders."

Pam looked like she was about to protest my usage of the term *marching orders* when Mina asked, "Are you going to take us to Calf Pasture Beach?" She took a long pull of coffee. "I guess they don't still have cows in your town."

James laughed. "Somebody did her homework."

"Well, I googled where you guys live before we came up. I like to know where I'm going," Mina said. "It must be beautiful along the coast."

I kissed the top of Mina's head, avoiding the chopstick, and headed to the sea-green guest bedroom to exchange my flannel pajama bottoms for a pair of corduroys.

So far, so good, I told myself. We were almost one third of the way through the visit; appearances would be maintained, harmony would reign and I might even be able to muster some holiday cheer that wasn't totally fake.

ஒஒ

My mother's announcement at Thanksgiving, that she and my father were going on a trip to the Holy Land over Christmas to celebrate their thirty-fifth wedding anniversary, accounted for our presence on Gregory Boulevard on December twenty-fourth.

I had been mildly curious, since my parents aren't particularly religious and their anniversary is in March.

"Dear, this is a *scholarly trip*, not a pilgrimage," Mom had said. She went on to explain that they were very lucky to have been accepted to join an exclusive tour group led by a pair of eminent academics, a historian and an archaeologist who were both from Princeton University and who had co-written a *New York Times* Notable Book sometime in the last century. This was such a special opportunity my parents simply had to go, even if it meant visas and vaccinations and leaving their offspring to fend for themselves during the festive season.

I wondered if Dad felt the same way, but he had clearly signed on for the duration thirty-five years ago, and the only thing I found to say was, "Sounds fun. Hope you guys have an awesome time."

Then my brother called the Tuesday before Christmas to ask if I wanted to spend the holiday with him and his girlfriend. "You know we're renting this house in East Norwalk so we've got plenty of room, and Pam's all excited to have a Christmas tree, make a big dinner. She wants to have *family* around."

"You're living with a Christmas-tree-hugger named Pam?"

"We moved in like six weeks ago. Jesus, you've *met*

Pam before. Remember we all had brunch at Mom's favorite place in the Village for her birthday? Actually maybe you don't remember. You were out pretty late the night before, you looked like shit, and I thought you were going to spew your Eggs Benedict. Anyway Mom's been to the house, and she loves her. You should read your frikking emails every once in a while."

I heard a beep.

"Sorry Chris, gotta take this call, let me know about Christmas, talk to you later, love you bro."

"Shit," I said, addressing the departmental contact list tacked to the pocked beige wall of my cubicle. "Shit, shit, shit." My plan to spend a subversive Christmas Eve getting trashed with my Jewish friends was seriously imperiled. My brother was living with someone, in a house, and despite a bit of pronoun confusion, it appeared that my mother approved of both the residence and the girl.

I was co-habitating with a spindly pot plant and a slew of cockroaches in a third-floor walkup, though thankfully I was sleeping with someone on a regular basis. James and I were four years apart and the sibling rivalry thing wasn't that strong between us. Even so, I could not envision stepping alone and forlorn-looking off the Metro-North train at Christmas, a figure of fun and pity on that suburban platform, with a giant "L" for LOSER hovering in the air above my head.

I really, really needed Mina.

෯෯

"You want me to spend Christmas Eve, with you, at your brother's house, in Connecticut?" Mina didn't sound actively hostile to the idea, just puzzled.

She had never met my family. We'd only been seeing each other for a few months; we hadn't exchanged keys to our apartments, were barely at the *I Love You* stage, and I'm pretty sure neither of us had said it sober.

"It'll be fun," I said feebly.

Silence.

I tried for a winning, vulnerable yet manly look. "Please, Mina, I so need your moral support or else I'm not gonna be able to get through this."

"What's up with the last-minute invite, Chris? And why do you even care about going if it's going to be such an ordeal?"

I wanted to describe my brother to her without making him seem like an arrogant jerk. "James isn't a big doubter. He's not like me. He's always sure where he's going, and now he's going to beat my ass in the race to becoming a responsible adult."

"We're twenty-six, we don't have to have everything figured out yet," said Mina. "And I never knew you were competitive like that." Her voice dropped an octave: "*My brother is going to beat my ass, oh woe is me!*"

"I'm not explaining it right." I waded on. "He's older, we're different, it's cool. But if he and the g-f have decided to host a major holiday, like our parents would, with real plates and different courses and everyone sitting around a dining room table, I have to show up and play my part." Entertaining for me could stretch to a roast chicken but it would have to be picnic-style, sitting on the floor and eating off the coffee table if there was more than one guest.

"And I'm supposed to be what, your beard? A witness to testify that you're a grown-up guy in a heterosexual relationship who is gainfully employed?"

"You're supposed to be my ally," I said. "My blessed, beautiful ally." And it must have been the right thing because Mina pressed her palms on my cheeks and leaned in to kiss me hard on the mouth.

"OK Chris, I need some more backstory here. Who

all's going to be there besides your brother and his girlfriend? Anyone who still believes in Santa Claus? What about gifts?"

Relief trickled through me. "It's not going to be a big group of Yuletide revelers, and no kids. Just my brother, James, he works at this hedge fund in Greenwich, and Pamela, not sure what she does, and her parents, Mr. and Mrs. Something or Other. James said we don't have to go crazy on the present front, maybe just pick up something for the parents. I was thinking a gift basket from Zabar's..."

"You are never going to make it all the way uptown to Zabar's," Mina said matter-of-factly. "Call and see if you can get something delivered, or else we can hit the Christmas Fair at Grand Central before we catch our train." She twined her long legs around mine, and I pulled her onto my lap.

"Thank you... Thank you... Thank you..." I punctuated each pair of words with a little kiss in the hollow at the base of her neck.

ॐ

The prep work that goes into putting a holiday meal on the table occupied the four of us all afternoon on Christmas Eve, and it was actually perfectly pleasant. I topped and tailed green beans and was taught how to use a lemon zester. James peeled and cubed a taupe pyramid of potatoes. And Mina set the table with a forest of crystal and baby poinsettia plants artfully interspersed between the place settings, while Pamela fretted about the enormous oozing red lump of beef. She trussed it, dusted it with flour, stabbed it with a pair of meat thermometers, eased it on and off a scale on the countertop, radiating anxiety.

During one of her round-trips between the kitchen

and the dining room, Mina asked, "Shouldn't we be singing *Deck the Halls* or something?" She held a cluster of water glasses in each hand.

"You're so right!" said James. "I did a Christmas playlist for Pam. I should put it on."

Pamela wanted to know what we listened to at Christmas growing up, and my brother and I shouted in unison, "The Mormon Tabernacle Choir!"

"My mother played Handel's Messiah in a loop," Pamela offered.

"You guys are so high-brow," Mina said. "My parents had an old 33 LP of Perry Como singing Christmas carols. It was the Miller family's Ho-Ho-Holiday soundtrack."

By six-thirty, the house smelled of roasting animal fat, all available surfaces in the kitchen had been wiped down, and we were liberated to change for dinner. I had brought the standard uniform: white button down shirt, grey flannels and a blue blazer, which suddenly seemed not quite festive enough. I was just wondering if James could lend me a red tie or some Santa suspenders when the doorbell rang.

"Hurry up, I think they want to put the coats in here!" I hissed to Mina who was standing in her underwear, holding up a pair of fishnet stockings as if to check for dropped stitches.

"Hold them at bay honey, I'll be right out," she murmured.

You know how they say you should always check out a girl's mother before you marry her, since most women eventually become their mothers? This would have been difficult if not impossible for Pamela, as her mother was a full foot shorter, with a brittle physique that had little in common with her daughter's (Pamela's muscular calves and open, hearty mien proclaimed her to be a woman who enjoyed both playing team sports and a daily five-mile run). But I could see Pamela's ash-blonde bob morphing into her mother's steely grey coiffure, and both women had the same wide-set, pale blue eyes with lashes and brows carefully darkened. Grooming was clearly less of a concern to Mr. Talbot, who had dandruff flecking the shoulders of his tweed jacket and wiry tufts of hair protruding from his ears.

Mina emerged from our room wearing a long, dark-red velvet skirt and a stretchy black top that did great things for her boobs, as the rest of us gathered around the coffee table, with its silver tray bearing champagne flutes and little bowls of salted nuts.

I had shared a bathroom mirror with Mina a dozen times, getting ready to go out or off to work, me shaving and bleeding from a succession of nicks, she wielding a variety of brushes, tubes and pots of powder. I knew objectively how smoky eyes were achieved, but her appearance in that bright room was somehow exotic and magical. Right then I wanted more than anything to be reflected in her kohl-rimmed gaze. I stepped toward her, and a cork banged behind me. Mrs. Talbot cried out, introductions flew around the room.

At the dinner table, Mrs. Talbot launched the first conversational sortie while James was sawing away at the roast beef. "We're delighted to have you with us, Mina dear, but won't you miss your own family at Christmas?"

"Well, it's nice to be part of a family Christmas at all since I couldn't go home this year. My parents live in Wisconsin, and it's too far to go for only two days. I just started a new job, and I can't take any time off yet." Forestalling Mrs. Talbot's next question, she added, "I work at Scholastic Publishing. I just got my master's in early childhood education from Columbia."

"And how did you and Chris meet?"

"We both live in the same neighborhood downtown, and we kept seeing each other around, as you do. I think the first time we actually spoke was at Starbuck's, but that's such a cliché I don't often admit it to people."

It was at Bar 288 at four a.m., just twenty-five minutes before we got naked and twenty-eight minutes before we had sexual intercourse for the first time, but never mind. Mina swept the table with a glowing smile, inviting everyone to share her amusement at the thought of two young people meeting at Starbuck's over a soy milk latte—so sweet and touching, so of the moment! I thought I heard Mr. Talbot give an avuncular chuckle before attacking his mashed potatoes.

This was great. I had the best girlfriend in the whole world! She was gorgeous, she was perfect, she could carry these people with her and paint our lives to seem endearing, maybe even admirable.

I drained my glass of wine and looked around the table for the bottle. Mrs. Talbot's glass was empty too, and I filled us both up.

"So where did you two meet—at work?" Mina asked my brother. Before James could finish masticating a mouthful of resistant animal protein, Pamela broke in.

"Oh no. I'm a hospital administrator, but one of my girlfriends works at Jimmy's firm, and she took me to their holiday party last year."

I'll bet she did, I thought. I'll bet your friend's the receptionist and you both got your tits out for the delectation of all those rich young hedge fund managers to kiss under the mistletoe. And good for you, you caught one.

Over the course of dinner, it was established that we were all members of the same tribe. Pamela and Mina had both been on the Babson College Junior Year Abroad program, in Rome and Paris, respectively, and several years apart, though neither got her BA at Babson. Mrs. Talbot was passionate about the mission of the Nature Conservancy and served on the board of their Connecticut chapter, while I worked as a legal aide at the New York City Parks Department. And Mr. Talbot and James had an animated discussion, impenetrable to the rest of the table, on what the Fed's next move was likely to be.

"I will not be joining you for the church service, as I am an atheist," I announced loudly after scraping up the last of my chocolate mousse.

"I'm an agnostic, and I will join with pleasure," Mina said. She crinkled her eyebrows at me and began to clear dessert plates.

"I think I'll stay here with Christian, and we can get better acquainted." Mrs. Talbot looked kind of tanked, and she didn't seem too eager to hear the joyful noise emitted by the St. Matthew's carolers. This was not how I wanted my evening to wind up, tête-à-tête with Mrs. Talbot. I'd had a confused idea of making out on the couch then dissecting the others with Mina, a plan which I'd neglected to mention to my girlfriend.

Pamela appeared tense as she buttoned up her coat, and James murmured, "Behave yourself," to me. The front door sighed shut, car doors slammed, and I was alone with Pamela's mother in the suddenly silent house.

We sat at either end of the oatmeal-colored sofa in the living room for a few minutes, then I got up and retrieved the flask from my duffel bag.

"Do you like Irish coffee, Mrs. Talbot?"

"Why yes, I believe I do."

I microwaved two mugs of the leftover breakfast Fair Trade brew, added a generous slug of whiskey to each and found some Reddi-wip in the fridge to top them off.

"This is very nice, Christian." The whipped cream had given her a slight moustache, but I wasn't sure how to tell her to wipe it off.

"Your young lady is quite the free spirit," said Pamela's mother. "Not like my Pam. She's much more conventional, and vulnerable as well, though she tries to hide it. I am extremely protective of her, and it would distress me very much to see her hurt in any way."

Was she trying to ask me if James was a bounder? Warn him, through me, against trifling with her daughter? Why didn't she talk to somebody else about this, for Christ's sake?

"She's my only one, you know. I wanted to give her a little brother, but we couldn't have another child."

I didn't want to know any of this. "Uh, you don't have to worry, Mrs. Talbot. James is a really good guy... honorable... takes his responsibilities seriously..." My voice trailed off before I could get to "excellent provider" and "comes of good stock."

She gave a bark of laughter and swatted my knee. "You're not such a bad guy yourself. Now go fix us some more of that delicious Irish coffee."

❧

I put a plaid blanket I found in the hall closet over Mrs. Talbot, who was snoring gently. One of her pearl earrings had come off and was nestled in her stiff, frosted hair, but I didn't feel like reaching in and retrieving it. I wanted to be out of that house, alone, emotionless.

I closed the front door after me and sucked in the thin, icy air. I felt more than a little drunk myself and got on my knees on the front lawn, crunching through a thin crust of old snow. Then I pitched forward and rolled over, spreading my arms wide on either side and looking up, trying to discern a constellation, a star, an aircraft tower through the scudding clouds.

I didn't get up when I heard a car pull in the

driveway. I stayed where I was as the garage door rose and people clomped into the house, their voices tinny-sounding. More conversational background noise, more doors opening and shutting, the sound of the Talbots' Buick starting up and slowly backing away, old voices calling "Merry Christmas" through rolled-down car windows.

James laughed when he stepped off the front walkway into the yard.

"Come on man, get up, that snow's not clean. The neighbors' dogs come over here to piss all the time, and there's probably a few stray turds lying around."

He reached a hand down and hoisted me up.

"Thanks for coming. I really appreciate it. I know you and Mina probably had way more exciting plans in the city, but it means a lot to have you here. Mina's a trip, you should have heard her belting it out in church."

My brother slung his arm around my shoulders, then turned and pulled me into a crushing hug. "I hope you're happy, Chris," he said, his breath warm in my left ear. "I just really want you to be happy."

ം⚬ൟ

The room was dark and I banged my shin getting into bed. Mina was lying silent but not asleep. She moved away when I tried to wrap my arms around her and spoon, our usual sleeping posture.

"I don't hate you or anything, Chris," she said softly. "But you can be such a fucking asshole. Those people aren't horrible, you know that. And everybody was trying to make it a nice evening. I can fend for myself if you leave me alone with your family, after begging me to come here. But I don't understand why you preferred to get an old lady drunk instead of being with the rest of us."

I fell asleep before I could think of anything to say in my defense.

The next morning, James was alone in the kitchen when I shuffled in.

He looked up from emptying the dishwasher. "Pam went for a run. I'm not sure if she'll be back before I have to take you guys to the train station, but she said to say Merry Christmas and all that."

"Tell her Merry Christmas too, and thanks for having us." I could hear water running in the bathroom. "I'm going to take a cup of coffee in to Mina."

"Why did I bring my cameraaaa / I didn't even take any pictures… "

Mina was singing quite low, in almost funereal, dirge-like cadences as she showered. I tried to open the bathroom door, but she'd locked it.

I sank down till I was sitting on the floor, with my back resting against the painted plywood door.

I'm going to get back to the city, and everything will be different. I'll quit my job and become a poet. My boss is going to wake up to my true potential and give me a fat raise and a promotion. Mina's going to dump me. We're going to mutually decide to go our separate ways. We'll get married, and she'll incarnate the new "hot bride" phenomenon with a dress that shows off her tattoos and butt cleavage.

I have no idea what's going to happen next, and I hate it.

Christmas Yet To Come

"Men's courses will foreshadow certain ends, to which, if persevered in, they must lead," said Scrooge. "But if the courses be departed from, the ends will change."
— Charles Dickens, *A Christmas Carol*

Survival of the Christmas Spirit

Aimee Horton

Christmas Eve

I stand in the dining room doorway and give a happy sigh of pride. Pulling my phone out of my pocket I snap a couple of pictures and upload them to Facebook, into my already bulging Christmas album. Now that the tables are all set for tomorrow's big dinner, I am finally starting to feel in control of everything. It looks better than I ever imagined; you can't even tell there are three different tables. What's more, unless you look really closely, you can't even tell that two of them are plastic outside furniture.

That's right, my dining room is filled with our normal dining table, two white plastic patio sets borrowed from my friend Jane and a last minute buy from eBay. If I'm honest, it didn't look great to begin with, but after much searching, the Internet came up trumps. Not only did I find a beautiful Christmas tablecloth that covered all three tables, but chair covers to match.

Leaning forward, I adjust the position of a tea-light

holder, and faff a pile of sequins shaped like holly out a bit more.

Perfect.

I'm so excited. It's my first ever time hosting Christmas, and I'm feeding eleven people. There's my mum and dad. My brother, Oscar, his wife, Laura, and their teenage daughter, Lexi. Then there's Henry's mum, Maria, and her third husband… Charles, I think. I can't keep up, to be honest. Finally there's us four. I've never cooked a Sunday roast for more than us lot let alone Christmas dinner, and somehow, eleven people are coming to witness it. But luckily it won't be a disaster; I've built a spreadsheet.

The kids have spent the day in front of the TV eating chocolates, and I've spent the day peeling veg and wrapping pigs in blankets. I've even had time to make an amazing chocolate log from scratch. All I need to do tomorrow is put things in the oven at the right times, and we're onto a winner. Even the presents are wrapped— usually we're still wrapping at nearly midnight. I can't believe how organised I am.

All that's left is for Henry to bring the turkey home tonight. Then we all snuggle up and read Christmas stories before putting the kids to bed, ready for Santa to come. While we're waiting, Henry and I are going to have wine and order in a pizza.

Not sure I can wait until tonight for something to eat though.

Suddenly, after all my hard work, I'm starving. I head into the lounge to grab a handful of Christmas chocolates, planning to crash out on the sofa with the kids for half an hour before I start cooking their tea.

Just as I'm unwrapping a green-foil-wrapped triangle of chocolate and deciding what topping to have on my pizza, my phone bings from inside my pocket.

Pulling it out, I try not to acknowledge how snug my jeans are, and instead look at the message on the screen.

NO WAY—I can't believe it. I close my eyes for a few seconds.

Why does my mother always make life difficult for me?

Opening my eyes again, I glare at my phone and re-read the message.

AUNT V UNCLE R HOUSE FLOODED. THEM MANDA JAMES AND TWINS COMING WITH US TO YOURS STOP. LOL MUM XXX

It used to take me ages to decipher my mum's text messages, but this one is as clear as day. At four p.m. on Christmas Eve, my mum has added six extra people—two of those toddlers—to the eleven I already have to feed. Oh, and she thinks LOL means *lots of love*, not *laugh out loud*—which would actually be more appropriate given the circumstances.

Two extra toddlers. That means three toddlers will be trashing my house while I'm cooking Christmas dinner.

Last time we had a toddler play date, all three had taken their nappies off and stuffed them down the toilet, nearly flooding the bathroom.

Dottie—focus. There are bigger problems than two additional toddlers.

There's not enough food.

Even though the turkey Henry is picking up is massive, there is nowhere near enough food for Uncle Rob's appetite. I've seen him devour a Sunday roast quicker than I can neck a gin and tonic.

I'm going to have to go shopping.

I can't imagine anything worse than the supermarkets on Christmas Eve but I have no other choice. After shoving a handful of kids' snacks into my handbag, I chivvy the children out the front door, through the pouring rain and into the car, tripping over the next door neighbour's cat.

Blooming thing is always getting under my feet.

The rain is rattling on my windscreen like Lego

blocks on my old glass coffee table—the one that had to go after Mabel head-butted it and bled all over the white carpet that we'd managed to keep clean all the way through the Arthur toddler years. I peer through the windscreen wipers, and in a last ditch attempt to avoid the supermarket, I head for a cluster of local shops around the corner, and pull into the disabled parking space right outside the butchers. Leaving the kids in the car, I leg it inside. The bell jingles as I enter the nearly empty shop, and a woman in a striped apron looks up from behind the counter. The smell of meat hits me, and I feel bile rising in my throat.

"Turkey?" is all I can manage to pant, looking hopeful. The woman laughs and shakes her head, so I turn and race back outside, calling "Thank you anyway!" as I go. I stand outside for a second, breathing in the fresh air before clambering back into the car, my damp hair stuck to my face.

"There's nothing for it," I say as I buckle my seatbelt. "I have to go to the supermarket." I head to the nearest. It's small, but hopefully that will work to my advantage.

Judging by the amount of cars in the car park, I can tell it hasn't. After coaxing the children out of the car with the promise of sweets, I walk through the automatic door, take one look at the line at the tills snaking its way around the store, and then turn around, narrowly missing bumping into a woman with a heavy dose of coral lipstick.

"I wouldn't bother!" I say jokingly, smiling at her as I usher the children back outside, already promising they can have *two* packets of sweets at the next shop.

The woman grunts at me, and carries on into the shop, just as a man dressed in a royal blue polo-shirt with the shop logo on it walks out and deposits a sign reading "NO TURKEY OR PARSNIPS LEFT" onto the pavement next to the trollies.

I hope she was looking for turkey or parsnips the mardy moo.

"Come on, monkeys, let's go. We still need to find that turkey and get those sweets," I sing to my grumpy children as we run back across the car park.

Next stop ASDA.

I let out a low groan. I know it's going to be packed. It always is, but hopefully they'll be on top of stock control.

I don't even bother heading towards the parent and child spaces. I abandon my car in what feels like the furthest space, near the petrol station and car wash. With a child on each hip, I run as fast as I can towards the store. There don't seem to be any trolleys available, so dragging the children behind me, I head to the fridges. No turkeys. We head to the freezer.

Nothing.

There are, however, some really cute looking mini pigs in blankets, so I pick those up, along with a couple of packets of sweets and two bottles of prosecco that are on offer.

Practically a saving.

The children are getting impatient, and I don't blame them. The queues go nearly as far back as the store does, and the kids have eaten two packets of sweets each before we've even made it to the till.

Glancing at my watch, I realise it's already past their dinner time. "You guys are being soooo good," I say, squatting down to wrap my arms around them, wincing at the wee smell coming from Mabel's nappy. "So so good!"

They grunt, not bothered by compliments. "Are you guys hungry?" I ask, and just as I catch their attention, the line moves forward. "We have another shop to go to." I see them beginning to wilt, so I hurry on, desperate to win them over. "So how about we stop off at McDonald's and pick up dinner?" I sing-song. The kids respond by jumping up and down and clapping. Relieved, I ease myself up, my knees creaking as I do. Suddenly though, I find myself sprawled out on my front, my two bottles of prosecco rolling across the aisle.

What the actual…?

"The line's moved," says a voice behind me. Turning round, I look up to see the woman with the coral lipstick from the last shop. Her trolley sits exactly where I had been crouched moments before.

"I can see that," I say, smiling as politely as I can, picking myself up off the floor. I send Artie off to retrieve the bottles. Just then, the woman in front of me realises she's forgotten kitchen roll and leaves the queue, meaning I'm next. We shuffle forward again, and before I know it, we've paid and are already back in the car driving towards McDonald's, knowing full well where we have to go next. The Superstore.

Eurgh.

I go through the drive-thru, and place the Happy Meal boxes on the front seat next to me, knowing that saving them until we're in the superstore is the only way to avoid a meltdown. A meltdown I can hardly blame them for.

Driving through the rain, still recovering from the woman with the awful coral lipstick actually knocking me down with her trolley, I wonder just how busy the superstore is going to be.

I snap to as the imposing blue, red and white sign of the supermarket looms over the road in front of me. Taking a deep breath, I turn into the car park.

I've never seen it so busy. I crawl along looking for a space, and as I move into my third lap, I spot one. Suddenly, as I also spot a sports car headed my way, driven by somebody who looks suspiciously like the woman with coral lipstick, realisation dawns. If everyone is coming with my mum and dad, that means they're staying at my house too. In my two-bedroom house.

Bugger.

Zooming haphazardly between the white lines, narrowly missing the convertible as it tried to nab the space first, I park wonkily and turn off the engine. *HA*. Pulling out my phone, I text Jane.

Mother strikes again. Can I borrow your airbed and sleeping bags? I send, before quickly sending another: *Buying extra turkey, will be around after that.*

Shoving the phone in my pocket, I climb out of the car and grab a nearby abandoned trolley, fighting against the suddenly gale-force wind. Unplugging both kids, I lift them into the trolley, iPads, game consoles and Happy Meals included. They complain as the rain lands on their screens, but I make a mad dash across the car park, and we are inside before any of us gets too soaked. Trying not to notice the carnage of the last-minute shoppers packed into every square inch of the store, I can't help but spot my enemy following me in. I square my shoulders.

Right. Turkey.

Without stopping to browse the homeware section like I normally would—although do we need extra wine glasses?—I push the trolley determinedly towards the fridges at the back of the store. With the exception of a lone chicken, the shelves are empty. I turn, bashing a few buggies and an old man on a mobility scooter out of the way (don't look at me like that, I'm pretending not to notice what I did), and head to the frozen aisle.

As I approach, I see there is one turkey left. The coral lipstick lady is coming towards it from the opposite direction. I look at her. She's about my mother's age, but more spritely. Abandoning my trolley and the children in the middle of the aisle, I race over and grab at it. Our hands lock around the ice-cold bird at the same time. I look at her. She stares at me. I swear she's gritting her teeth. I open my mouth, about to explain my predicament, sure she'll understand.

However, she's on a mission. This woman, with her stupid lipstick, and her Marks and Spencer leather gloves. This woman, who has already knocked me over once. She yanks the turkey so hard I have to let go. I fall back into the aisle, landing inside the trolley containing my two small children.

"Excuse me!" I call, clambering out in a rather un-lady-like fashion. "Excuse me, I really need that! I have four extra adults and two toddlers coming for dinner at the last minute… Their kitchen is flooded!" I totter after her as she marches down the aisle in the opposite direction. "Please!" I say as I rub my sore back and bruised calves. She doesn't even turn around, and I realise it's a dead loss.

No Christmas Spirit there then.

Standing in the middle of the frozen aisle, I try to decide what to do. Another supermarket is going to be just the same. There's only one thing for it: sundries. Slowly, I turn around and head back towards the fridges and the tiny chicken, grabbing boxes of powdered gravy and stuffing as I head to homewares. Only new wineglasses can save us now.

§

Arriving home, I'm pleased to see Henry opening the front door as I park the car. Kissing my head, he opens the boot stuffed with sleeping bags and pillows from the ever-reliable Jane.

I plop the children directly in front of the television. The batteries on their electrical devices died at the till in the supermarket, but after a slight incident with a nearly stolen bag of brioche, the reminder that Santa is on extra-special watch while he's packing his sleigh was enough to keep them both quiet.

I'm unpacking the shopping when Henry brings in the last load. He drops it in the hall and circles his arms around my waist. I lean back and give him a kiss.

"I've done something… I hope you don't mind," he begins, standing in the door of our dining room. My stomach fills with panic. I hate it when he makes executive decisions.

"Okayyy?" I say, bracing myself, but not wanting to look worried.

Stepping aside, Henry waves his arm towards the dining room, which leads into the conservatory. The conservatory door is open, and the little table from Artie and Mabel's bedroom is now taking pride of place. It has a tablecloth and a variety of toddler-proofed table decorations, including electric tea-lights.

"How did you… ?" I begin, and notice the main table has been shuffled around as well. It looks amazing and accommodates everyone.

"Cut up a spare chair cover." Henry beams with pride.

I feel a wave of emotion and burst into tears. Sobbing, I run into my bewildered husband's arms and cry for what feels like forever.

"Sorry," I murmur into his shirt when I'm finally done. "I just thought we'd never fix it, and I have a stupid small chicken and hardly any food, so I didn't know what was going to happen, then you do this, which is lovely." Then I start crying all over again.

Henry smooths my hair and pushes me to arm's length, probably to save his shirt rather than to check if I'm OK.

"The turkey is huge, the chicken will be fine. Kids hardly eat anything, and as long as you have extra Yorkshire puddings, you'll be set." He smiles that smile he does to reassure me. "Now," he says, checking his watch. "Let's shove some food down the kids and get them into bed so we can open that new gin my boss gave me."

"No need to feed them, I got them McDonald's." I beam, not only pleased at my own forward planning, but at the opportunity to inhale half of their Happy Meals.

Bolstered by the thought of the gin in the snazzy bottle, we get the children bathed and dressed in record time.

Well, when I say "we," I mean "Henry." I stay in the kitchen, making some last-minute alterations to the timetable for tomorrow.

There weren't that many alterations to make really, just add "put chicken in oven" half way down the timetable. But I really couldn't be arsed with the bath-time meltdown I knew would happen with an overtired Mabel and an over-excited Artie.

After tweaking the timetable, I rummage in the cupboard and pull out a bag of kettle chips. The strong salt and vinegar ups my energy level, and as I hear the water gurgle out of the bath, I take a deep breath and make my way slowly up the stairs in time to see Henry dressing both children in their matching Christmas pyjamas.

I grin. I always like them at the end of the day, when it's nearly time for them to go to sleep.

"Let's read on Mummy and Daddy's bed tonight!" I say, and together we all bundle under the quilt and read *The Night Before Christmas*. Mabel snuggles in close to me, sucking her thumb, her eyelids already drooping, while Artie on the other hand can barely sit still.

He's going to be trouble.

As we close the book, Henry scoops Mabel into his arms and takes her across the hall, leaving me with a hyper Arthur.

Sneaky sod.

"When is Santa coming?" he asks, bouncing up and down on my bed. "I'm going to see him, you know! Will he come in my room? Where's my stocking? If I put it under my window, he'll wake me up if he takes it out to fill it up." He fires off the questions in quick succession, making me regret leaving the bowl of chocolates in front of the CBeebies Pantomime.

I don't even begin to answer. Instead, I pick him up and cuddle him, carrying him into his bedroom, hoping that once he's in there, with an already fast-asleep Mabel, he will be quiet. "Shhh now, nah night, I love you." I lean forward, stroking his head.

"But I have tummy acheeee," he whines quietly into my hair.

"No you don't," Henry whispers over my shoulder, pulling the duvet up to Artie's neck before making a hasty exit.

Glaring at his departing back, I lean in to give my son one last kiss, and he wiggles his arms out and around my neck. "I can't get comfortable." His eyes are wide and innocent—a giveaway that he is totally lying about everything.

He's excited. I should give him a break.

Sighing, I sit on the edge of the bed and try not to think about my lovely gin and tonic going warm and Henry having full control of what pizza we're ordering.

"Santa only comes when you're asleep," I begin, stroking his hair. "So snuggle down, and think about the lovely songs from the Christmas films you've been watching."

"But I can't sleeeep."

"Yes you can. You haven't even tried."

"Noooo, I want to see him. Can I just come and kiss Daddy one more time?"

I lose patience. I'm hungry, tired and really want a drink.

"Artie, snuggle down and go to sleep. I don't want to tell Santa to take your presents off the sleigh." I play my trump card, even though I'm aware it's far too early.

"You wouldn't do that. He's already in the air. He's already flying his sleigh. You told me so earlier."

I knew that bloody follow Santa app would stuff up my evening one way or another.

"Look Artie, this is your last chance," I say pulling out my phone. I've started it so can't stop now. "Go to sleep, or I'm going to text him."

I kiss him and turn to leave the room.

"If you message him while he's flying his sleigh, he might crash and die," my son says quietly from under his duvet. "Then you'll have killed Santa."

Give. Me. Strength.

"Then I'll call him," I say, although I know I shouldn't respond. I should just walk out of the room and down the stairs, but I can't help myself.

"Does his sleigh have hands-free, then? Because Daddy says if you use the phone while you're driving you could crash." I swear there's a meaningful pause before he says, "Don't worry though, Mummy. I haven't told him you text and speak to Auntie Jane while you're driving."

The little…

"Yes, it has hands-free," I say, forcing a smile. "Now go to sleep." I begin walking towards the door again and as I hear my son start speaking, the sound of the phone ringing downstairs rescues me.

"Mummy has to get the phone. GO. TO. SLEEP and DO NOT wake your sister," I say, louder than intended. Then I race down the stairs to answer the phone before it rings out. It's my brother, Oscar.

He speaks first, before I even have a chance to say a word. "Hello, how are you doing?" I realise I don't have the energy to rant.

"Thanks for rescuing me from bedtime hell," I begin, before answering his question. "As well as can be expected, I guess." I slouch down onto the hall floor and lean against the wall. Accepting a gin and tonic from Henry, I wish once again we'd gone for a cordless phone instead of a retro-looking one. I look like a moody teenager on the phone to her boyfriend.

"I mean, what can I do?" I ask. Knowing he has no answer, I go on to list what food I have, and Oscar—who's a plumber—goes on to explain about the pipe that was under the flooring in Auntie V and Uncle Rob's kitchen, and how they'd been staying at my mum's all week.

I'm not really paying attention—too busy seething at my mother's short notice—when my mobile phone beeps from within my jeans pocket. Pulling it out, I swear without even meaning to.

"FOR FU—"

"What's the matter?" Oscar asks, stopping mid-flow in his explanation of stock cocks or something similar.

I re-read the text first to myself and then out loud to my brother.

DON'T FORGET MANDA AND JAMES ARE VEGGIES—TOLD THEM YOUD DO THEM NUTROST LOL MUM XX

"She told them I'd do them a nut roast?" I say in disbelief, taking a glug of my gin and wrinkling my nose in disgust. Either the new stuff is horrid or the tonic is different, because my usually favourite drink tastes vile.

Does my mother hate me?

"I can't actually believe she actually promised them an actual nut roast, and left it until seven-forty-five p.m. on actual Christmas bloody Eve when I haven't even had a chance to order my bloody pizza yet! Can you believe it?" I squawk down the phone at my brother. He doesn't say anything.

"Oscar? Are you listening to what our bloody mother has done?" I raise my voice, and Henry races in and points up at the stairs, reminding me we want the children to be asleep, not stay awake. I lower my voice and whisper, "Oscar?"

"Dots, you're in luck!" My brother is smiling, I can tell by his voice. "Lexi's boyfriend, you know the one who's in a blooming band of all things, he's a veggie. She says she can make something and bring it!"

I hear the voice of my sixteen-year-old niece in the background, and I want to hug her.

I'm just about to shower her with compliments when Oscar continues, "She also says she has some special gravy you can use." I sigh with relief. I hadn't even thought about different gravy, and tears of relief prickle in my eyes.

"Tell her she's amazing, and I love her, and I am just about to pop something extra into her Christmas present." I sniffle down the phone to my brother as we say our good-byes, confirming they'll be here for Buck's Fizz around eleven a.m.

Still feeling emotional, I spend a couple of minutes looking at the dining room to cheer myself up before seeing if Henry has ordered our dinner. All that talk of vegetarians has given me a hankering for a vegetable-topped pizza.

He's not in the lounge, and as I wander across the hall to the kitchen to see if he's there, I hear voices upstairs. Peering upwards I see my husband's long legs stretched across the landing opposite the bathroom door.

Artie is obviously having a delay-sleep toilet-visit.

Going to replace my gin with a glass of red wine, I spot Arthur's iPad on the counter and realise Henry is only halfway through the pizza order.

Oh my God, I'm starving!

I add a few more bits to the order and then, spotting

an offer at the top of the site, I add an extra pizza and garlic bread to get an additional twenty percent off. Now we'll have enough for leftovers on Boxing Day as well. Turning to my overflowing wine rack, I choose a bottle of my favourite red, two wine glasses, and on a whim, I also grab the half-eaten bag of kettle chips from earlier.

I settle down on the squishy sofa in the lounge and put my feet up on the table, relieved once again that everything that can be done today is done. All that's left, once Artie is asleep, is to take the presents upstairs and fill the children's stockings.

I turn on the TV, switch the channel from some high-pitched, brightly coloured kids' animation to a rerun of *Home Alone 2*, then set to work on the rest of the crisps. Munching my way through a couple of handfuls, I am thrilled at how festive the room looks. The tree lights are twinkling, the logs are crackling in the fireplace, while the Christmas candles burn next to it. I can't help but get excited all over again about the thought of tomorrow, with everyone in here opening presents and enjoying themselves. I close my eyes for a minute and imagine if we had a piano how I could play Christmas carols and everyone could sing, like a really old-fashioned Christmas celebration.

Not that I play the piano, but still.

Just as I'm deciding whether I should go help Henry with Artie—who is trying every delay tactic in the book—I hear footsteps on the stairs. When Henry walks into the lounge, the doorbell rings.

"Perfect timing, honey!" I let him answer the door, not intending to move again until the stocking-filling and bedtime.

"How much did you order, Dots?"

I turn to look at my husband. Perhaps I did go a bit overboard. You can only see the top of his bushy hair over a pile of about eight, maybe nine, boxes.

"I've been a busy girl!" I exclaim, rubbing my tummy before clearing a space on the coffee table. Laying out a couple of old magazines to protect the wood, I continue over-justifying. "Plus, I thought leftovers for Boxing Day maybe?"

"My wife, classy as ever." He smiles, setting down the pile of boxes and ruffling my hair. I dive into the food, opening sauces and grabbing a bit from each box.

Settling back onto the sofa, I bite into my pizza, and as I begin to chew, my throat closes up.

Urgh.

I take a sip of wine and let the liquid soothe my throat and settle my churning stomach.

I'm still sweaty and weak, so after taking another sip, I grab a handful of crisps from the bag on the floor. The sharp flavour does its job and I begin to feel back to normal. Tentatively, I reach for a potato wedge, but can't quite face a chicken dipper.

It must be those cold fish fingers I'd snaffled from the children.

I look at the slice of pizza on my plate and the nearly full boxes in front of me.

"I'm full," I say, setting my plate on the floor.

"You shouldn't have wolfed down an entire bag of crisps." Henry rolled his eyes good-naturedly. I attempt to look shocked.

As he clears the food away, I head up to check on the children. I'm exhausted, so exhausted I can barely climb the stairs, but as I walk into their bedroom, a rush of energy runs through me. Even though it's only nine p.m., both of the children are fast asleep. I'm thrilled.

Grabbing their stockings, I whisper down the stairs to Henry, and together we sneak into our bedroom and stuff them. Tiptoeing back into their bedroom, we put the stockings at the end of their bed, not daring to kiss the children in fear of waking them up. Finally, I go back to my bedroom to put my pyjamas on.

Dressing gown wrapped around my still not-totally-settled-stomach, I spot next door's blooming cat curled up on my pillow. It must have snuck in when Henry answered the door.

Bloody thing, look at the mucky paw prints all over my duvet!

Scooping it up, I lecture it quietly as I trot down the stairs. I open the front door and gently evict it. Feeling slightly guilty, I remind myself of my now dirty bedding. I head back into the lounge to watch the Take That Christmas special and have a last glass of wine before Henry finishes the bottle.

Christmas Day

I can't believe I'm the first person awake, especially after Mabel woke up at two a.m. and started unwrapping presents. Luckily, I heard her before it was too late and managed to re-wrap them. Hopefully it was too dark for her to see what she'd got.

Now, when she is nearly always up before six a.m., here I am, lying in bed at six-forty-five, and the house is silent. Well, except for Henry's snoring.

I lie there, straining my ears over the snorting next to me, for sounds of the children waking up. I'm excited to hear the squeals of their voices when they see Santa has visited. In fact, I'm so excited I feel sick.

Unable to keep still, Henry's snoring irritating me more and more, I go downstairs and pop the oven on. It will be good to get a head start and have it ready for the turkey to go in after breakfast. After flicking on the kettle, I check my colour-coded itinerary. Satisfied I'm on track—five minutes ahead actually—I grab a mug and open the fridge for the milk. I beam with pride at how well stocked it is.

I love a full fridge.

I make my tea and take a sip. It tastes gross. Gagging at the horrid taste, I spit what's left in my mouth right back into the mug. Eurgh, the milk must be off. Wrinkling my nose, I tip the liquid down the sink, and just as I'm about to wash the mug, something twitches in my brain.

Wait.

Slamming the mug on the counter, I spin around and fling the fridge open again. There's no turkey.

Bloody Stupid Idiotic Henry. I can't bloody rely on him for anything.

Racing up the stairs, taking them two at a time, I descend on the still-snoring lump in our bed, shaking his shoulder.

"HOW COULD YOU FORGET THE TURKEY?" I yell, not caring if I wake the children. "How could you be so idiotic to forget the bloody turkey?"

Rolling over, my husband looks at me through half-open eyes.

"What? Huh? What?" He croaks, brushing his slightly wild hair out of his eyes. It takes all my willpower not to pick up a pillow and beat him with it, before having a full blown Mabel-style tantrum on the bedroom floor.

"The. Turkey." I begin, through gritted teeth. "You were meant to pick up the turkey."

"I did!" Henry replies, eyes fully open now. And suddenly realisation dawns on him. "I left it in the boot of the car!" He looks relieved that he's back in control of the situation. "It was so cold last night, and I knew the fridge would be overflowing, so I left it in the boot."

"Oh," I say, feeling a bit guilty. "Thanks."

How was I supposed to know that?

I head quickly down the stairs, grabbing the keys; I'm now desperate to get the turkey inside and safe. I'm hit by the freezing cold morning as soon as I open the door, although I can't help but enjoy the winter sun on my face. *Perfect Christmas weather.*

Unlocking the car, I heave the huge bird out of the boot, somehow managing to close it again, before I stagger inside. Dumping the turkey on the kitchen counter, I turn to close the front door, but before I get there, a gust of wind catches it, and it slams shut on its own accord.

The noise wakes the children, and within seconds, shrieks of excitement echo through the house. I make my way upstairs to join in.

৶৻৶

"No, you can't have chocolate for breakfast," I say over my shoulder to a grumbling Artie, as I make my way to the kitchen. I see Henry sneak Artie and Mabel chocolate coins, and I smile to myself.

"How about a mince pie instead?" Mabel instantly claps her chubby, chocolaty hands together in delight, and Artie fist pumps the air in agreement.

Happily, I leave the room, humming my favourite Christmas song—Mariah Carey, if you're interested—as I go. My stomach is rumbling for a mince pie and a fresh cup of tea. Once I've had that, I can really get cracking. We're still ahead of time.

As I reach the kitchen, I stop and stare at the scene in front of me.

"NOOOOOOOOO!" I try to scream as I stand in the doorway. However, it just comes out as a choked whisper.

On the floor, in front of the fridge, is the turkey. Well, I say turkey, but what I should say is the *remains* of the turkey. On the windowsill, looking out over the garden is next door's cat, licking its lips.

I don't believe this.

"Henry!" I call, in a strangled voice. "HENRY!"

My husband lollops across the hall, and without me having to say anything, the smile falls from his face.

"What the actual…?" he begins, and then stops, turning to look at me. I assume he's trying to assess how I'm coping with the situation.

"We're screwed," I say, the panic setting in. "We are totally and utterly screwed." I stamp my feet on the spot and let out a frustrated growl. Launching across the room I practically yank the cat off the windowsill, then march to the front door with it held at arm's length. I'm furious with this animal.

The children have appeared behind me, wondering what the commotion is all about. "Was the cat bad?"

Artie asks. "Maybe he should go on the naughty step," he suggests, ever the helpful one.

My anger subsides—slightly—and I plop the cat onto the ground. "AND STAY OUT!" I shout, slamming the door behind me. Brushing my hands off, I feel marginally better.

The feeling quickly fades as I see Henry picking shreds of raw meat off the floor. Artie and Mabel trail behind me. I grab a packet of mince pies from on top of the breadbin and pass it to Arthur.

"Kids, go into the lounge and watch TV and play with your new toys, will you?" I say, in a high-pitched sing-song voice. I was going for upbeat and in control but failed.

As they scarper across the hall, whispering and giggling at the opportunity to sneak more than one mince pie, I look at the kitchen, nearly clear of the evidence.

"What are we going to do?" I ask, shoulders slumped.

Henry hands me another cup of tea, but the smell of it turns my stomach. I set it on the counter. "The milk's off," I say, with a dramatic arm gesture. "Just ANOTHER thing to add to the list."

"Tastes OK to me," he says, shrugging before returning to the rather more serious matter in hand. Christmas Dinner.

"We could call everyone," he says, putting his arm around me. I rest my head against him. "They could all chip in and bring something. I'm sure your mother has a frozen joint in the freezer."

Urgh. My Mother.

"I can't think of anything worse than admitting to my mother that I've failed." But I know his suggestion is probably the only option.

"Do we have anything in the freezer?" he asks, and I shake my head. I'd cleaned out our tiny freezer only a week or so before in preparation for the big day.

Opening the fridge, Henry and I stare at its contents, which this morning looked bulging and full, and now look pathetically sparse. The three large pizza boxes containing the remnants of last night's meal are stuffed above the salad tray—mocking me and taking up valuable space, which could have been filled with extra pigs in blankets and roast potatoes.

"Pizza?" he suggests, half laughing.

"I'm calling Oscar." I stomp into the hall and pick up the phone, hoping my brother—or at least his daughter—will come up with another magical solution after last night's nut roast miracle.

ৡৣ

Unfortunately, this time my brother was unable to work miracles. In fact—once he's done laughing—it's clear the only solution was the one Henry had come up with.

I'm going to have to ask my mother for help.

So now we're not having turkey, but we have an assortment of various main courses, which I hope will go with the vegetables. Along with the nut roast, Laura and Oscar are bringing a cottage pie and chicken. Maria is bringing a joint of gammon, and my mother, along with a whole load of judgement is bringing some "nice sausages and a portion of sweet and sour chicken." It might not be the most conventional of Christmas dinners, but at least there should be enough for everyone.

We're going to be OK.

Now it's twenty minutes before everyone is due to arrive, and I'm showered, dressed, and attempting to tweak my well-thought-out spreadsheet, replacing things like "baste turkey" with "put cottage pie in the oven."

The house is unexpectedly calm, and I feel as in

control as somebody can be when their—what I consider to be gourmet—Christmas dinner plans are turned upside down.

It's going to be fine.

Just as I'm getting ready to make another batch of Yorkshire pudding mix, the doorbell rings. Without even having to open the door, I know my mother has arrived. I don't know how, but I swear the doorbell sounds stressed and anxious. Just how she makes me feel.

Before I have a chance to prepare myself, the door is open, and our tiny hall is filled with people. My children squeal with excitement at the bags of presents in my dad's hands. I greet everyone as the twins belonging to Amanda and James burst into terrified squeals at the unexpected noise and unusual house.

"Why don't we all go into the lounge?" I suggest, starting to worry how everybody is going to fit into the small room.

"DARRLINGGG!" My mother sweeps in, handing me two rather-on-the-small-side, freezer bags. "What a catastrophe! I was so looking forward to turkey. We've even been having beef on Sundays to build up to the bird." She takes the glass of Buck's Fizz Henry has offered her and kisses me on each cheek. "I should have known when you mentioned you had a cat this would happen."

"Dirty horrible creatures," my dad says, turning to Henry and asking for a "man's drink" instead.

"It's not my cat," I say, for what feels like the hundredth time that day. "I told you on the phone. It's next-door's. It keeps sneaking inside."

"Well you shouldn't encourage it," my mum says.

Changing the subject, I look at the freezer bags.

"So erm… How many sausages do we have?" I ask my mother.

"Four. And a portion of the sweet and sour. Make

sure the chicken is heated right through." I'm about to question how many people she thought we were feeding when she says, "That's one good thing at least. No turkey means at least she can't poison us all." She then makes her way into the lounge and repeats the exact same sentence to Val and Rob.

"I need a drink," I say, but before I can open the fridge, the doorbell rings again. As soon as we open it, the house is officially full. Henry's mum, Maria, and Charles are here, somewhere behind two massive bin liners decorated with tinsel. And behind them are Oscar, Laura and Lexi. The twins, who had just calmed down, start screaming all over again, and Mabel shouts at them to shut up.

A wave of nausea flows through me, and I take a deep breath before leaning in for kisses.

Henry's mother fusses with my hair and hands both children what appear to be life-sized replicas of puppies. "They are just the same as real doggies, except you have to plug them in to charge every night," she tells the children, as the one that looks like a Dalmatian does what looks suspiciously like a toy poo on the floor. A white poodle with a pink bow starts yapping loudly.

"I need a drink," I say again, and this time, as if by magic, my dutiful—and for once, very helpful—husband is by my side.

"Gin?" he asks, opening the fridge and reaching in for the tonic.

"You know what?" I say, my stomach lurching. "I actually fancy a Tango—is there one cold?"

Giving me a strange look, Henry rummages in the bottom of the fridge and pulls out a can. He's just opening it for me when Oscar comes in carrying foil dishes with cardboard lids, a large freezer bag and a frozen-solid pack of chicken thighs.

"Voilà!" he says, placing them on the kitchen

counter. I grab the Tango from Henry as he leaves with two cans of beer for our guests. Gulping it back, I am relieved as the sugar hits my system.

That's better.

"No gin?" Oscar asks, opening the fridge, and reaching for a beer for himself.

"Nah, don't fancy it for some reason," I say, removing the lids from the foil containers and looking in despair as I realise that yet again, they're portions for two people, not nineteen.

"Not like you," my brother says, and then he laughs. "Last time you were off gin, you were pregnant with Artie."

Laughing, I punch him on the shoulder shaking my head.

"Daft sod. It's just stress," I say, although something starts to tick in the back of my head. But then my mind flicks back to the dinner ahead.

"Everyone likes Yorkshires, yeah? I don't need a special oil or anything for the vegetarians, do I?" I reach for the eggs and flour. "Go on through, I'll be there in a second when I've just mixed this batter—then we can exchange gifts."

It takes me two minutes to mix another jug of batter, then I stick the chicken in the microwave onto defrost.

Taking a last slurp of fizzy orange, I grab a champagne flute and head into the lounge in time to see Artie open a massive Spiderman remote control car from Oscar, and Mabel a Range Rover ride-on that needs charging up before she can ride it. Henry disappears for a few moments, returning with a couple of extension wires and multiple plug sockets.

I can't believe my two-year-old daughter has a Range Rover before me.

"We're going to have to buy a new house just so we have room for all these toys!" I say, and Henry rolls his eyes.

"Any excuse to bring up a house move!" he says, and I beam at him innocently. I've wanted to move for a while. It would be nice for the kids to have their own bedrooms now that they're getting older. And as much as I love our little terrace, the kitchen is quite old. Plus a laundry room so I don't have to hide the ironing on our bed when we have visitors would be amazing.

Just as I begin to dream about double garages and an en-suite, I hear my name behind me.

"Dottie!" I turn to see Val beaming at me, a gift bag in her hand. "I'm so sorry to land us all on you at the last minute." She hands me the bag. "Here you go. It's not much, but your dad assured me you'll love it!"

Opening it excitedly—I love a good present—I pull out a bottle of my favourite gin, complete with branded glass, and a little bottle of tonic. "Oh Val!" I say, "You shouldn't have!" I give her a hug, then head into the kitchen and set the bottle on the counter. Squatting down, I open the oven door and check on the chicken.

For such a small bird, it seems to be cooking slowly.

In fact, the oven doesn't feel that hot. Turning it up a bit, I jiffle some of the baking trays so I can slide the Yorkshire puddings in. Then I set the time so I remember to come back when the oil is hot, before finally checking the chicken in the microwave. It's starting to defrost, but I put it on for another ten minutes just to make sure it's totally thawed.

God I'm hungry.

Reaching into the cupboard, I feel about until I find the nearly empty bag of kettle chips from last night. I stuff a handful of crumbs into my mouth, then another and another. God they taste good.

Just then, I hear a rattle of a plate. Uh oh. The chocolate log I'd so lovingly created had been placed on top of the microwave, probably when somebody was rummaging about in the fridge looking for drinks. Without even looking, I know what's happened. Sure enough, as I carefully pull the plate down, my beautiful chocolate log is a puddle of chocolate sauce and curdled Bailey's cream.

I look at it in despair, my eyes prickling with tears, as Henry races into the room with an empty bottle. He reaches for the kitchen roll.

"Don't panic," he says. "But my mum spilt some Buck's Fizz on the carpet, and your mum cleared it up with the red paper napkin… "

I don't want to look. I only had the carpet cleaned the other week, and already Mabel took her dirty nappy off on it, and Artie spilt a glass of Ribena over it. Taking a deep breath—come on Dottie, man up—I grab a dish cloth, and with a smile plastered on my face, head to the lounge.

The two women, obviously already the worse for wear after God-knows-how-many glasses of Buck's Fizz, are giggling like a pair of school girls on the sofa. And as my mother sees me, she sticks her foot out in a hurry, using it to cover the pink stain on the carpet.

"We can't take you two anywhere, can we?" I say, forcing myself to laugh. I leave the room without even bothering to clean the stain on the carpet. I dump the remnants of the chocolate log in the bin and stand at the sink counting to ten. By the time I get to nine I feel a hand on my shoulder.

"Don't worry about it, love," says Henry soothingly. "I've Googled it and found a solution. We'll nip to the shops tomorrow. If everything's calm in here, why not join us for a second? Come and watch the kids trying to play TWISTER. It's hysterical."

Henry, ever the positive. But he's right. "I'll be there in a minute," I say. I put the defrosted chicken in the oven, and while I'm there, I shake the pigs in blankets and reset the timer. Then I put the cottage pie in the microwave to defrost and check the meatloaf, which is reheating in the slow-cooker. Finally, I grab my glass and head into the lounge where Artie is trying to do left arm green.

It's lovely, actually. The rug has been pulled over the stain, and my lounge is filled with laughter. People are lying on cushions on the floor or curled on the sofa, and the children are laughing hysterically as Lexi attempts to help Mabel do left foot yellow. Although I smell a strange odour coming from over by the twins.

My sister-in-law's glass is empty, so I grab a bottle of wine and top up her glass. As I set the bottle down, I see a trickle of yellow running down one of the little girls' legs.

Please no!

"Er… Amanda!" I squeak, indicating to her daughter. She jumps and scoops up the child, catching the yellow liquid in her hand. "Bathroom's upstairs," I say.

God, I can't wait for Mabel to be toilet-trained.

Cringing, I head back to the kitchen. This is the final run. The Yorkshire pudding, gammon, and cottage pie all need to be in at the same time, and soon the chicken will be out, and we can all sit down. Most of the vegetables are roasting with the chicken, the sprouts are on the hob, and the gravy is ready to go in the microwave.

Considering this morning's disaster, I think it's going to be OK.

It won't be perfect, but it will be fine.

Except—oh God no—I open the oven door and reach in for the tray of oil, and instead of the burning heat making my arms prickle, cold air does.

Flicking the heat up and down, I realise I can't hear the fan either.

Shit. Shit. Shit.

Walking as calmly as I can across the hall, I poke my

head into the lounge. "Hen?" I say, keeping my voice surprisingly level even though I can feel the bile rising in my throat. "Can I borrow you for a sec?"

Henry stands up and makes his way into the kitchen, and as soon as we are out of earshot, I whisper, "The bloody oven is broken!"

"What?" We squat in front of the oven, wafting our hands in and out, turning it on and off at the wall. That's when we realise the microwave is silent, and the light on the slow cooker is off.

"Shit!" he exclaims.

Oscar pokes his head in. "Everything alright in here? We appear to be having a slight electrical fault in the lounge."

Great.

Henry and I head back to the lounge. Everyone seems oblivious to the fact that the lights are no longer on.

"What happened?" I ask my brother, who tells me he went to unplug Mabel's car and it hadn't charged, and nothing else had either.

We go from room to room, trying various plugs and sockets. They're all off on the ground floor.

It's just the fuse gone. Dinner will be delayed, but it's OK.

Henry and I check the fuse box in the downstairs loo using my phone as a torch. Sure enough, the fuse switch for the downstairs is off.

Phew.

Henry climbs onto the toilet, and balancing precariously, flicks the switch back on. I wait for the lights to turn on and the noises to begin, but nothing happens. I try the light switch. Nothing.

Shit.

"Try it again," I say, desperately, and Henry does. He flicks the switch up and down about five times before climbing down from the toilet.

"It's broken."

What are we going to do?

"What are we going to do?" Henry asks, echoing my thoughts. "I'm guessing dinner isn't cooked enough?"

"No, no Yorkshire puddings, none of the meat is cooked through and most other bits were due to go in the oven ten minutes ago," I say in despair. "The potatoes and carrots and stuffing are under a not-yet-cooked-chicken so I doubt they're safe."

"So what do we have?" Henry asks, and even he is beginning to look totally defeated.

I think for a moment. "I guess we could reheat the meatloaf, nut roast, and sprouts in the microwave upstairs on the landing?" I suggest, thinking that it didn't sound very appetising.

"Just meatloaf, nut roast and sprouts?" he asks, as we make our way into the kitchen. "With gravy?"

I open the fridge and pull out three boxes. "And pizza."

❧

Candles lit, everyone is gathered around the dining table laughing. Laid out in front of us are plates filled with microwaved pizza, breaded chicken and wedges. There are also bowls of Brussels sprouts, nut roast, meatloaf and dishes with frozen garlic bread slices, which have been cooked in the toaster at the top of the landing.

I can hear the chatter in the dining room while everyone takes their places and corks being popped out of bottles of wine. As I'm carrying the last plate of breaded chicken out of the kitchen, I foolishly pop a piece in my mouth. All of a sudden I feel sick. Quickly, I force the plate into a passing Henry's hands and run upstairs to the bathroom. I empty the contents of my stomach down the toilet before leaning over the sink and washing my mouth out, panting.

When the feeling subsides, I sit on the closed toilet with my head in my hands. I really can't do with being poorly right now. It would ruin today. Because despite all the mishaps, it's been lovely having everyone here.

I lift my head, ready to brace myself and go back downstairs. As I do, I catch sight of a nappy bag in the bin, and my stomach lurches again. This time with fear instead of nausea. Oscar's passing remark about me going off gin flashes into my head, and I remember I couldn't eat chicken when I was pregnant with Mabel. I start to work things out on my fingers, and as I do, realisation slaps me in the face. I quickly lift the toilet seat and hurl again.

I'm pregnant.

Shit. Shit. Shit. I can't think about this now. Standing up, I shake myself and wash my face. I reapply make-up for good measure. Slowly I make my way downstairs and join my guests.

Henry is standing at the head of the table, holding a glass of champagne. As I sit next to him, he hands me my glass and makes a toast.

"To Dottie, who against all odds, the neighbour's cat, the last-minute guests, the supermarket stalkers, and the blown-out fuse, has made us a wonderful dinner, and given us a fabulous Christmas I'm sure we'll never forget!"

That's for sure.

"To Dottie!" everyone says. "Cheers!"

Together we raise our glasses, and I set mine down without taking a sip.

"No champagne, Dots?" Rob asks, laughing.

"Oh, I'm just hankering after a slice of pizza—let's eat already!"

"No gin and no champagne!" Oscar exclaims. "That's not the Dottie we know and love. Come on girl, get it down you!" he says, topping up my glass.

Henry is still standing. He's been topping up people's glasses, but he's now looking at me.

"No booze, off chicken and eyes bigger than tummy..." he says, slowly. I cringe as I see realisation dawn. I shake my head, hoping he'll catch on that this isn't the time for this.

He doesn't.

"You're...?" he asks, sinking into his seat.

"I think I am..." I nod looking wearily at him, trying to pretend that there aren't seventeen pairs of eyes on us.

"But how?" Henry asks.

Oscar bursts out laughing. "I don't think we need that at the dinner table now do we Henry?" Then pushing his chair back, my brother takes the stand. "To Dottie and Henry—for making this a Christmas we'll never forget!"

"A Christmas we'll never forget!" Everyone laughs, their glasses held high. Except my mother of course, whose lips have formed a disapproving line.

And with that, my stomach flips again. This time, because I can't imagine how the hell I'm going to cope with three children when I can barely keep two alive. I take a swig of my champagne, spitting it out as I remember I can't drink any more.

It's going to be a long few months... pass the pop.

Chris Aftermaths

Didier Quémener

North Region, Confederate Lands
Gateshead, ex-England – December 5, 2321

The decades of drought hollowed out the River Tyne to the depths of its soul. Only the two great arches of the Millennium Bridge remained. Proudly they stretched their rusty forms to the sky from their bed of cracked earth, baked by the burning sun.

Hand to his forehead, chin tilted up, Chris' gaze met the highest point. In his other hand, he held a wooden box that had endured the ages, from generation to generation. Its markings illustrated the hardship of the past centuries and the conflicts that had left a trace not only on objects but also on the lives of men and women.

"Find the triangular diamond and bring it to the foot of the bridge! When the two arches meet, you will know what to do…"

The last words of Chris' grandfather reverberated like a persistent enigma in his mind. Mystery wasn't a stranger to Chris. His whole life sometimes seemed like one big question mark. Orphaned at a young age, he was raised by his grandfather. Speaking of family was taboo. Everyone—including Chris—knew the old man by the name "Smart Trash Chief." And watch out if you addressed him by any other name!

Smart Trash Chief was a man of few words. His grumpy character and bad moods were known well beyond the frontiers of the North Region. He was proud of his unpleasant temperament and didn't try to hide it.

Even as Chris stood before this desolate picture, this scene that hadn't been touched by a raindrop in years, he still couldn't help but imagine how all had looked before. He closed his eyes. He thought of green, rolling hills, animals running free, villages, people… And then his thoughts darkened, returning to reality. The few stories his grandfather told, the old manuscript showing the progressive destruction of all forms of modern technology, the desert-like fields as far as the eye could see: All of this flooded his mind. He immediately opened his eyes to block the dark images. But facing the grim scene in front of him, there actually wasn't much difference between the view eyes open and the view eyes closed.

Chris decided to examine the contents of the box Smart Trash Chief left him. Sitting on the base of the bridge's pillars, he set the container on his knees. His heartbeat accelerated.

"I'm being idiotic," he said aloud. "Why would I be afraid of what's inside?"

The box was big enough to hold a pair of children's shoes. In black ink across the top was inscribed "Chris Aftermaths." Chris lifted the lid.

A sheet of paper was folded in half, its contents hidden. Chris opened it and read the following message:

-- -.-- / -.. . .-. .-. / -.-. .... .-. .. ... ---... / ..-. --- .-.. .-.. --- .-- /

- .... . / -- .- .--. .----. ... / .. -. .... - .-. .. .-.- -.-. - .. --- -. ... / .- -.
-.. / -- .- -.-. . / -- . / .--. .-. --- .-- -.. .-.-. .-.-. .-.-. / -.-- ---
..- / .- .-. . / --- ..- .-. / .-.. .- ... - / -.-. .... .- -. -.-. . / .- -. -..
/ .. / -.- -. --- .-- / -.. . . .--. / .. ..- / -- -.-- / .... . .- .-. - / -
.... .- - --..-- / .--. .... . .-. . / .-- . / .- .-.. .-.. / ..-. .- .. .-.. . -..- -
-..-- / -.-- --- ..- / .-- .. .-.. .-.. / .... ..- -.-. -.-. . . -.. .-.-.-

Morse code was the Confederate Lands' only written language, but used by so few that it was close to extinction. It seemed like a last symbol of virtual unity, yet it masked a much darker reality—that of a people torn apart.

The text presented no challenge for Chris. Quickly, he read the following:

My Dear Chris:
Follow the map's instructions and make me proud. You are our last chance, and I know deep in my heart that, where we all failed, you will succeed.

Without much attention to Smart Trash Chief's note, which was as obscure as his final words, Chris continued to explore the contents of the box. Two small brown paper sacks, one on top of the other, caught his eye. When Chris shook one of them, he heard a dry, sandy sound. To the touch, the texture was grainy, like rice.

"What does he expect me to do with rice?" he asked, sighing. "As it is, we don't have enough water to survive. Wasting it to cook a few grains of rice won't improve our situation!"

Chris ripped open the bag, and tiny black balls, the size of poppy seeds, slipped through his hands and fell to the bottom of the box.

"Shit! What is this mess?" He examined the back of the bag and read the following words:

Seeds for the South Region

Intrigued, Chris grabbed the other packet and looked for an inscription. The second one was marked:

Seeds for the West Region

"Yeah, we're going to go far with two bags of seeds, Smart Trash Chief! Is this for real? Some legacy from the head of a region!"

Chris lifted a small book with a brown leather cover from the box. The title gave him hope he might discover an intellectual treasure:

..-. .- .. - ....

He recognized the word "Faith." But in paging through the book, Chris realized that the volume would be about as useful as the bags of seeds.

Great, Chris thought to himself. *This gets better and better! The book is written in the Latin alphabet. I don't know of anyone since the scholars more than three centuries ago who can read these letters or understand this language.*

Chris set the book down and found a map in the box. It was the one Smart Trash Chief spoke of before his last breath. The map showed four regions: North, South, East and West. On the map, someone had sketched a picture of the book in the East Region. The rest of the map, made of a rough, dry chamois material, was covered with inscriptions that were difficult to decipher at first glance. The marks resembled dried blood.

Chris returned his attention to the box. At the very bottom lay a photo, positioned face down. Chris, extremely curious, scratched at the wood to unstick the picture. It was a color photo, yellowed by the passage of time. The portrait was of an old man with a long white beard and bushy white hair. He was plump and wore round glasses. He was wearing a red suit.

"OK, we're not going to solve our problems with this mess of useless objects," Chris grumbled as he returned everything to the box. *I'll look at the map in more detail in the morning. Now it's time to go back underground.* The wind whipped up, announcing an electrical storm, as Chris tossed a final glance at the bridge.

North Region, Confederate Lands
Gateshead, ex-England – December 6, 2321

The night was short for Chris Aftermaths. Stretched out on a worn cow's skin, he'd spent hours, map in hand, trying to understand the mission Smart Trash Chief had left him. In spite of their differences and the generations that separated them, Chris was determined to honor his grandfather's memory. Just twenty, Chris had neither the experience nor the confidence to take a leadership position, but he was courageous and set on fulfilling his responsibilities. The map indicated the South Region as the first destination.

Chris grabbed his sunglasses and backpack, and set off, like a vagabond wandering through unknown territory. In his bag, he carried Smart Trash Chief's box and a syringe filled with the universal treatment. Chris stopped at the foot of the Millennium Bridge and looked at it solemnly.

"Smart Trash Chief, alias Grandpa, I will make you proud!" he called out. "You won't be disappointed. You'll see."

Chris arrived at the gates separating one region from the next and presented the underside of his wrist.

"Chris Aftermaths, descendent of Smart Trash Chief, on a secret mission," he said, his voice arrogant as he spoke to the supervisor.

"Matriculation number 54.945/-1.6175—Third Generation," read the man in a black suit. He entered the information into a small glass plaque, and luminous symbols flashed across the surface.

"You are free to pass. Where are you going, Matriculation number—"

"Chris, my name is Chris Aftermaths," he interrupted. "Don't forget that! We are not matriculation numbers, understand? We are the present and the future, and we have to do everything we can to end this life without a future. Do you see that? Can you read it?"

Chris lifted his sleeve and revealed the tattoo on his forearm.

> *Yours is the light by which my spirit's born: (…)*
> *-you are my sun, my moon, and all my stars.*
> E.E. Cummings

The man stared at Chris' arm as he gripped the young man's wrist. In a split second, his expression changed.

"I… I'm sorry!" he said, discomfort in his voice.

Chris had no idea why these words, tattooed there at his birth, always had the same effect on the supervisors. He remembered, as a child accompanying Smart Trash Chief during his nomadic trips, his grandfather would roll up Chris' sleeve at each checkpoint. As if by magic, the doors would open without even the slightest question.

"Forget it—it's fine this time," Chris said, his tone insolent. "Now use the only technology remaining in this world to send me here." He pulled out his map and pointed to the South Region.

"I have to meet The Rich Mr. Fat Ass, and I'm in a hurry."

The man didn't flinch. He opened the rectangular bag attached to his belt and grabbed a metal handle. Then he pressed a button, and a synthetic voice spoke: "Enter the address of your destination, matriculation number and password. Stand in transportation position, and close your eyes."

"Are you ready for the molecular transfer?" asked the supervisor.

"Go ahead," Chris replied.

The man hesitated for a fraction of a second before the final step, entering his fingerprint.

"You… You're not closing your eyes?"

"I'm not afraid of death. I don't believe in leaving like a coward. Scan your finger, and I say to you, 'see you soon.'"

The supervisor did as he was told. Chris took a slow, deep breath. He felt like he was suffocating. His chest tightened, heat filled his body, and less than five seconds later, a sensation of heaviness tugged at his legs.

Sadness overwhelmed Chris as he gazed at the scene before him. The earth, to its very depths, displayed a face damaged by centuries without a trace of humidity. Crevices of more than five feet sank into the dirt, like doorways to Hell. Even the light of three suns burning interminably wouldn't dare penetrate them. The holes, somber and sharp, seemed to wait for one thing: to vacuum innocent victims into nonexistence.

"This isn't going to be fun and games," Chris murmured. "A real obstacle course."

"That's where you're wrong. We've been waiting for you."

Chris turned abruptly. His hand touched the case enclosing his syringe.

"Don't worry," said the young woman standing in front of him. "No one is sick here. It's the West Region that is being destroyed by epidemics. Here, we're only dying of hunger. Slowly but surely."

"Who are you?" Chris asked.

"Well to start with, let's say 'hello.' We are civilized, you know. I'm Ocarina Jade Mini. Pleased to meet you."

Chris looked Ocarina Jade Mini up and down. Camouflage pants, threadbare denim jacket, black curly hair. The young woman's face reflected all of the daily challenges of life in this hostile territory.

"I'm—"

"I know who you are. Don't wear yourself out with explanations. So you like my hair?"

Chis, startled, remained speechless.

"I'm asking because for the past two minutes, you haven't looked at anything else. OK, now come on, hurry up. They're eager to meet you."

"Who?"

"I'll tell you on the way." She hopped on a red bicycle and looked at Chris. "Get on," she ordered.

Chris settled on the luggage rack, and off they went, the bike squeaking intermittently.

"Are you all right back there? Hang on. We'll be going down fast, and it might be bumpy!"

Chris gripped the luggage rack with one hand and held the box against his body with the other as Ocarina Jade Mini lowered her shoulders over the handlebars. And they began a wild race to the village at the base of this gigantic fissure in the earth. There, at the bottom, sat about forty rickety old houses.

"This is our destination?" Chris asked.

"Exactly! It's no palace, but it's all we have. And in any case, the earthquakes and cracking of the ground destroy everything, so there's no use in rebuilding. You've been here before, haven't you?"

"Yes, a long time ago. When I was a child."

"That's what The Rich Mr. Fat Ass tells us. You'll meet him."

Chris' expression hardened. He was going to get to the heart of the matter. Both anxious and impatient, Chris wouldn't pronounce another word until they arrived in the village center.

In front of a crumbling wall surrounding one of the homes, a man awaited. He was tall, with broad shoulders and a square jaw. Chris jumped to the ground before the bike rolled to a stop. He hung back for a minute or two, always on guard.

"You have nothing to fear. We knew you would come."

"You're The Rich Mr. Fat Ass?" Chris asked.

"Yes. So that wise old owl Smart Trash Chief has left us?" His tone was a bit sardonic.

"You want to lose your life, old man?" Chris snapped. "If that's what you want, you've got it. You don't intimidate me."

"Stop, Chris!" Ocarina Jade Mini said. "We've all seen so much misery for generations. Both of you, stop."

Chris took a step back. Slowly, the adrenaline settled, and he recovered a calm sense of control.

"You're right. I'm here to honor the mission my grandfather gave me. I don't want to waste my time with you."

"You will stay here today and follow our way of life. We'll talk about everything in about twelve hours. Now, let's all go to our caves for rest from the sunlight."

The villagers who had been watching retreated one after another.

"Come on, Chris," murmured Ocarina Jade Mini, "you can share mine. I have a million questions to ask you!"

Chris followed. He lay next to her, and the hours of rest imposed by The Rich Mr. Fat Ass passed as if they were simply a few minutes. Ocarina Jade Mini hadn't exaggerated; she posed an endless stream of questions. About the organization of life in the North Region and about Chris himself, his teenage years and the time spent with his grandfather. She already knew so much about him, and Chris knew nothing about her. So she told him how Smart Trash Chief and her great-uncle, The Rich Mr. Fat Ass, had been in conflict for years, and that in spite of their responsibilities as heads of regions, they took great care to avoid each other.

Ocarina Jade Mini told him how, like everyone in the North Region, those of the South survived on dehydrated food and that the ancient pills three times a day replaced water. But even with all of their efforts, the villages' populations were waning, and the extinction of their race was on the horizon.

Footsteps outside.

"It's time," a man said. "He's waiting for you."

Ocarina Jade Mini and Chris left the cave and walked to the center of the village. Thousands of people, many from far-flung areas of the region, filled the square. The Rich Mr. Fat Ass stood in the middle on a stone table.

"Southerners! Southerners!" he called out. "Listen to me! Our suffering has lasted for much too long."

People yelled, sang, clapped their hands.

"Today, I offer you a savior! Today, I present you with the hope of a people! Today, I announce to you a new era..."

"What's he talking about?" Chris asked Ocarina Jade Mini.

"Shh, Chris, he's talking about you!"

Chris almost fell over. What other fantasies was The Rich Mr. Fat Ass going to come up with?

"He's here, among us. Finally! Welcome him, my friends, let him hear your voices! Chris Aftermaths has come to our village!"

The cries bubbling up from the crowd made Chris dizzy. To make matters worse, the heat and the light were so intense that even sunglasses did little to protect him.

"Make room, let him come to the center!" shouted The Rich Mr. Fat Ass.

Chris felt like a pawn as he stood next to the chief of the South Region. Not quite knowing what to do, he mechanically held out his grandfather's box. The crowd fell silent.

"Go ahead. They know you have something for us. Something for humanity!"

Chris lifted the lid and seized the packet labeled "Seeds for the South Region." He had carefully closed the package with an elastic band the previous day. Now he presented it to the crowd and announced, "People of the South Region, here are the seeds!"

Women and men gyrated wildly while young children began to cry, frightened by the agitation around them. Following the instructions on the map, Chris gave the seeds to The Rich Mr. Fat Ass, who immediately accepted them. He removed the elastic band, asked the crowd to move aside, and with a swift flick of the wrist, threw the seeds to the sky.

"From these insignificant seeds, will come life!" he proclaimed. "Herbs, fruit, plants, flowers, trees, vegetables... Our martyrdom has reached an end, people of the South! In a little less than three weeks, we will be free!"

Astonished by the scene, Chris sought out Ocarina Jade Mini. Tears streamed down her cheeks. He was about to run to her, but The Rich Mr. Fat Ass held him back.

"You will see her again soon, Chris Aftermaths. Have faith in me."

Then the Rich Mr. Fat Ass rolled up his sleeve to reveal the following inscription:

The owl of Minerva spreads its wings only with the falling of the dusk.
G.W.F. Hegel

"Remember the day when all will change, Chris. Remember my words. Now, leave. A great battle awaits you in the West Region. The people there have a life even worse than ours."

Chris' eyes locked with those of Ocarina Jade Mini, and in a fragment of time—hardly even that of a single breath—he saw The Rich Mr. Fat Ass scan his wrist. He hadn't even realized that the man had been holding his hand.

Chris disappeared before the Southerners and the damp eyes of Ocarina Jade Mini.

North Region, Confederate Lands
Gateshead, ex-England – December 7, 2321

"Already back?"

Chris lifted himself up slowly, turning his back on the North Region's supervisor. For the first time, a feeling of melancholy washed over him. Under normal circumstances, Chris wasn't used to falling victim to wayward emotions, but this time was different. He had one obsession: returning to Ocarina Jade Mini as soon as possible.

"Don't go too far," Chris said to the man without looking at him. "I'll be back in a few hours."

He could have traveled to the West Region right then in order to accomplish his mission, but Chris' curiosity about the diamond grew with each second that passed. He waited for some sort of sign from his grandfather above. He searched for an explanation. But his effort was in vain.

The only clue: "Find the triangular diamond and bring it to the foot of the bridge."

For starters, I need to know where to look for it, he thought as he gazed in the direction of the Millennium Bridge. A heavy silence set in, reminiscent of the moments following an electrical storm. Wanting to complete the two remaining visits as quickly as possible, Chris returned to the supervisor.

"There's no time to lose. Direction: the West Region!"

"Are you sure? I mean—"

"Do your job," Chris said, cutting him off. "I didn't ask for your advice."

The man followed his orders, and the ritual began. The same sensations coursed through Chris' body as during the previous trip.

Gathering his energy, Chris turned to look around. In

spite of three suns at their highest point, the thick layer of gray clouds made the air suffocating. An acidity lingered in the air and burned his throat. Eyes protected by sunglasses, Chris took a white tissue out of his pocket and covered his nose and mouth.

The ancient map vaguely indicated an area of importance. Chris started walking, but stopped almost immediately. His foot sank into a soft surface that hardened under pressure. A feeling of horror filled his heart. Chris was walking on a body, spread out, face down. To the left of this body, was another, and then another, two in front, a third behind… Dozens, hundreds, thousands of bodies as far as the eye could see. This apocalyptic vision terrified Chris, and paralyzed by fear, he remained frozen to the spot. He stayed that way for several minutes, his eyes widened behind their glasses.

"They drop like flies. A frightening rug, isn't it?"

Chris nearly jumped at the sound of the voice.

"I think this would be a good time to use your syringe, Chris Aftermaths, before it's too late," the man added. "They're contagious."

Chris hadn't noticed this man, who had been standing before him since his arrival. Hypnotized by the morbid exhibit, Chris had difficulty forming words to address him.

"I don't understand," he finally said. "Where have I landed?

"The syringe, Chris, the syringe! I don't have anything to protect you. Use it, and quickly!"

Mechanically, Chris extracted the syringe from his bag, dropped the cap to the ground and positioned the needle over his carotid artery.

"What are you waiting for? Do it!"

"But why are you alive? How have you escaped this?" Chris asked.

"Later, the explanations. Later, if you're still around

to hear them. The longer you wait, the more harmful the side effects will be. Possibly irreversible."

In a state of panic, Chris didn't bother analyzing the situation. He drove the needle of the syringe firmly into his skin and closed his eyes. He'd never been frightened before this. He'd bragged about facing death without trepidation. But for the first time, his legs trembled, and his body went numb.

"You'll feel better in two or three minutes. You'll see."

"Who are you?" Chris whispered.

The man, sturdy and round, approached him.

"Assault Can. Head of the West Region, or what's left of it. Do you feel better?"

Chris nodded and opened his eyes.

"The Rich Mr. Fat Ass just informed me through the universal signal of your imminent arrival. If you are here, I presume Smart Trash Chief is no longer among us?"

"No," Chris said, his voice flat.

"Take my hand. We will go to a place that is a bit less grim."

Chris obeyed without the slightest resistance.

In an instant, the two men arrived at the foot of a mountain. The summit, veiled by pollution and acid rain, melted into a black cloud.

"Stick out your tongue and taste. You won't risk a thing. The injection immunized you. Taste the water of death, taste the misery we have created in our world!"

Assault Can raised his arms to the sky.

"Why?" he asked. "Why so much hate, so much ferocity toward our people?"

A bolt of lightning created the illusion of natural lighting around Chris and Assault Can. The electricity hit the ground, projecting rocks as hot as lava in all directions. The crater left in its wake, spewing smoke, was the size of the Millennium Bridge.

"What luck we haven't seen this sort of divine anger at Gateshead!" Chris said.

"The strikes are so frequent and so precise that I can tell you when and where they will fall in the moments to come," Assault Can said. "A diabolic exactitude."

Chris tried to take control of the conversation so that he could finish his task as soon as possible.

"Frightening, that's for sure." He fumbled through his bag. "I have something for you."

Assault Can stopped him.

"Not so fast! I know you have seeds for us. I know old Smart Trash Chief only wanted to do good by sending you here... Lest we forget him! But you aren't going to get away that easily."

Perplexed, Chris studied the chief of the West Region.

"You Northerners have it good," he said. "You're lucky. I don't care if they're dying of hunger in the South, if they are depressed in the East, or if in the North you're delirious with joy at the idea of bringing the Confederate Lands back together. Do you know what it's like to die a slow death because you can't breathe after just a few years of life? Do you understand? Do you want to know what I've seen since I was born? A small group of 'the lucky ones' and me? We are the last generation of the vaccinated. Do you know what that means? It means we remain alive to witness this human horror unfolding before our eyes. We are helpless! Each new generation is decimated before the age of twenty. It's been going on for centuries! We see them born. They carry the hope of life, of healing. And we see them fall, one after the other."

Attentively, Chris listened to each word. Assault Can's voice softened.

"All that you breathe, all that you touch, all that is around you and me is going to die," he said with a sigh.

"Everything is contaminated, and there isn't a cure."

A small group of young people, seemingly coming from out of nowhere, gathered around Chris and Assault Can.

"Look at them, Chris! Look deep into their souls. They've never known anything beyond this putrid scene."

Chris saw the sadness, the desperation. Behind his sunglasses, tears filled his eyes. Overtaken by rage, by uncontrollable anger, he jumped onto a rock and screamed at the top of his lungs, "People of the west, your misery will soon be over. This nightmare is going to end. Believe in me. Please, you have to believe me!"

He opened his box, removed the bag labeled "Seeds for the West Region," tore open the packet and tossed the grains onto the rocky soil.

"Patience! In a little more than two weeks, come back here to meet the chief of your region. Keep up your hope, believe in humanity once again!" His final words were solemn.

A little blonde girl of about four or five approached Chris.

"What are the seeds for, sir?" she asked innocently.

"My name is Chris, Chris Aftermaths. And you, what's your name?" he said, touched by her wide blue eyes.

"Duly Icon. Papa says the seeds are for nothing. He said you'd come but that won't change anything."

"Your papa is mistaken, Duly Icon. Trust me! Soon, these seeds will turn into plants, as if by magic. You'll see! When the plants grow leaves, you'll eat them. And they will make you strong and keep you healthy. The plants will become trees so tall that their branches will chase away the black clouds, and the sun will warm the land with its bright rays."

Duly Icon's mouth formed an "o" as she looked at

Chris.

"What are plants and leaves, Chris? And what are trees and branches?"

Chris had no idea how to answer such questions.

"Now, do you see the extent of the repercussions of our miserable existence?" Assault Can asked. "Now, do you understand?"

"I like you a lot," Duly Icon said to Chris. "Since you gave us something, I'll give you a gift too."

She reached into her coat pocket. Chris came down from the rock and knelt before the girl. She extended her small fist.

"Here, this is for you."

"You don't have to give me something, Duly Icon, you know. It's not—" And then he stopped.

"Go ahead, take it!" she insisted.

Duly Icon had opened her fist. On her palm, an object shined. A triangle, sparkling in spite of the darkness of its surroundings.

"My papa gave it to me. It's called an 'adamas'!"

Chris lost his voice for a moment. He couldn't believe what he was seeing.

"Where did you find this diamond, Duly Icon?" he finally asked, his voice overflowing with joy.

"I told you my papa gave it to me. Be careful you don't lose it!"

"I promise."

"It's time to go, Chris," said Assault Can, placing a hand on his shoulder.

Exactly as The Rich Mr. Fat Ass had done, he rolled up his sleeve and showed the words tattooed on his arm:

In faith there is enough light for those who want to believe and enough shadows to blind those who don't.
Blaise Pascal

North Region, Confederate Lands
Gateshead, ex-England – December 8, 2321

Chris hadn't slept well. Nightmares, hallucinations and sensations of freefalls into black holes filled his night. Side effects of the injection were likely the reason. In spite of his fatigue, he had to carry on, to accomplish his mission. Since he had the diamond, he couldn't resist the temptation to return to the bridge and try to understand the enigma left by Smart Trash Chief. Chris hurried to the base of the arches, and pacing, reflected while repeating his grandfather's words over and over:

"When the two arches meet, you will know what to do…"

Chris racked his brain, but all remained obscure, all questions lacked answers. He caught a glimpse of the supervisor, who called him over with the wave of a hand. The man looked panicked.

"You must hurry! Another storm is approaching, and my energy resources indicator is weak."

"No problem," Chris replied, his tone nonchalant. "A final trip, this one to the East Region, and my travels are over."

"All right, here we go!" exclaimed the supervisor, who had begun to enjoy the activity of the past days.

Chris was eager to meet the East Region's chief. His map indicated the exact location. And as a matter of fact, the descriptions of this last region were the clearest on the map, as if the possibility of not finding this final meeting point absolutely had to be eliminated.

On a giant altar, curled up like a snail in its shell, a man sobbed. In front of him, lower down, hundreds of people on their knees were also crying.

"Are you the chief of the East Region?" Chris asked. *Talk about a leader*, he thought.

The man didn't lift his head. "Yes… Yes, that's me if

you'd like." He continued to cry.

"What's your name?"

He didn't reply.

"Come on now, get yourself together!" Chris said, annoyed. "Your name?"

"Slash… Slash Inaction."

"There you go. That wasn't complicated! What's happened here? Oh, and by the way, can you stop whining? Don't you see you're bringing everyone else down? It's not all rosy in the other places I've visited these past few days you know."

Slowly, the chief rose. Behind him, the walls of an immense building were covered with books as far as the eye could see. A giant tapestry of pages and words in many languages. This library was so gigantic it could have contained the history of all humanity.

"Have you guessed?" Slash Inaction asked as he wiped away his tears. "You see all of these riches? There is enough to feed the spirit of mankind for millenniums to come!"

"What's the problem, then?" Chris found himself losing patience.

"Is it that difficult to understand?" the chief replied, his voice aloof. "We have lost all knowledge of languages. All knowledge, all history. Our history—and not one of us is able to decode it! We are blind before this great mass of books. The wise men are no longer with us, and with their departure, they signed off on our demise. We don't know how to do anything but read. Read and teach the knowledge to future generations. And yet we can't. Today, we have lost hope. We have nothing left to teach, nothing left to wish for."

Chris remained still for a few seconds, then replied.

"It's not that bad," he said. "There's much worse in this world, believe me!"

"The misery of one isn't defined by comparison with

the misery of others!" Slash Inaction snapped. "Each one carries his or her own sadness. Everyone has a cross to bear! Look at them." He pointed at the people on their knees. "Go ahead. Take a look. Just try to comfort them if you're so smart!"

But Chris didn't say a word. The men and women looked like marionettes, puppets with disjointed limbs. Like a flock of lambs before their shepherd, they lingered here and there, lifting a head from time to time to make sure their leader was weeping as they were.

This time, we've reached rock bottom, Chris thought to himself. *If I give them one more book, they'll never recover. I can't be responsible for driving them completely over the edge!*

"What did you bring us, Chris Aftermaths?" Slash Inaction asked. "If you are here that means something has happened to my old friend Smart Trash Chief, doesn't it?"

"Old friend?" Chris asked, surprised. "You knew each other? I don't ever remember coming here to the East Region with my grandfather."

"Smart Trash Chief was my brother."

His legs shaking, Chris sat down. He felt faint.

"What? My grandfather was your... your brother? So we share the same lineage, we're from the same family? I didn't know I had an uncle or anyone else for that matter! Why hadn't we ever met?"

"A great-uncle to be exact."

"Whatever! It's not the time to give me a genealogy lesson."

"So the others didn't reveal a thing?" Slash Inaction murmured.

"Reveal what? Speak up now! What's this about?"

Chris was about to burst with anger. What he hated most was being manipulated in a situation he couldn't control.

"The chiefs of the other regions, The Rich Mr. Fat

Ass and Assault Can, they are also your great-uncles. We are—well we were, as your grandfather is no longer with us—brothers. The four of us were brothers."

These revelations pushed Chris into emotional overload. His feelings shifted from joy to annoyance. Why had they hidden the fact that they were family? Why hadn't they joined forces, combining their strengths to face adversity? So many questions ran through Chris' mind, and he was determined to obtain the answers, no matter what. Then, like a flash in his mind, he thought of her: Ocarina Jade Mini!

Slash Inaction understood by the look on Chris' face.

"I can read it in your eyes. You met your cousin, didn't you? You will see her again soon. It is written as such."

"It's written in one of those books you can no longer read, you or any of the others?" Chris couldn't hide his sarcasm.

"I understand your pain, Chris, and I don't resent you for it. Better days lie ahead because you are here before us. How old are you, son?"

"Twenty. But what difference does that make?" Chris stood up, but the old man stopped him.

"Sit, please. It's better that way. You want to learn history, our history? Maybe you aren't yet looking for the truth, but I can give it to you anyway…"

"Tell me!" Chris demanded.

"Very well." Slash Inaction took a deep breath and began his story. "According to the collective memory that we share, a young man will make an important visit in the year 2321. The wise men also left word, several centuries ago, that December twenty-fourth of that year, a new era would begin. The darkness weighing on us would disappear, water would soak the three suns, the storms would calm, and a blanket of white would cover the Confederate Lands. The next day, on December twenty-fifth, we would see the light of day. Men would see the purity of the sky, women would be fertile, and humanity would reunite. The young man is you, Chris Aftermaths. You must accomplish your mission, your destiny, to save us and to save humanity."

His great-uncle's revelations were not enough to satiate Chris' curiosity.

"But why didn't you use molecular transfer to find one another and fight together? By joining forces, you would have saved yourself decades of misery. Wait a minute, what am I saying? Centuries of suffering! What use in transmitting this collective memory from generation to generation without doing anything?"

"You're still so naïve. Young, sharp and courageous, but naïve! Everything seems easy when you speak to us, doesn't it? And when you addressed the people of the South and West regions, everything happened so naturally. Am I correct?"

"Well, yeah. Yes, like we're speaking right now."

"The luck of fools! You don't recognize your gift, Chris Aftermaths? You don't even hear it."

Chris knitted his brow.

"You are the only one to share our languages, the only one to understand all of us. Conflicts of the previous centuries punished us, inflicting us with a sentence that touched man to the depths of his soul. We are too evolved to be animals but too low to truly be human. Our punishment, what we all carry in our hearts: We share the same collective memory, but we can't communicate with one another. The North Region doesn't understand the South, which doesn't understand the West, which doesn't understand us. Our languages no longer link, Chris. Our cultures don't connect. You are the only tie between us. You understand the words of everyone, down to the idioms and slang of every region, without even realizing it."

Chris removed the book from his box. The crying had stopped, and people stood around him.

"Maybe I speak all of your languages without realizing it, but I'm incapable of reading this!" He held the book out to Slash Inaction. "The only thing I understand is the word written on the cover because it's written in Morse. It means 'faith.'"

An elderly man approached, his spindly legs shaking. "He has the book, the universal book! Let me through. He has the book! Let me see it before I pass on. Then, I can go in peace."

Chris moved toward the man.

"What's in this book? Tell me!"

Not without difficulty, the fragile figure finally made his way to Chris.

"Our destiny is in your hands."

"That seems to be the case," Chris murmured, a touch of sarcasm in his voice.

"The codes, young man, the codes! Written in the Latin alphabet, in this book, are the codes that only I may read and decode. The codes to all of the languages in history, in all of the regions. The codes that existed before the Confederate Lands. Thanks to this book, I will be able to read everything and teach. We can start over again! The walls of this building will no longer lie mute. Knowledge will spread like an epidemic of goodwill. Do you understand, my friend?"

Then Slash Inaction spoke, "You know the routine by now?"

Chris nodded.

The chief of the region rolled up the sleeve of his velvet simar. On his forearm, read:

As soon go kindle fire with snow, as seek to
quench the fire of love with words.
William Shakespeare

Men and women formed a circle around the old man, who read aloud. Slash Inaction pressed a button on his device, and Chris vanished before their eyes.

North Region, Confederate Lands
Gateshead, ex-England – December 24, 2321

More than two weeks had passed since Chris' visit to the East Region. In that time, neither storms nor heat prevented him from remaining in front of the Millennium Bridge. He sought an explanation—in vain. Fatigue won out. He was in a state of exhaustion. For hours, days, he waited, holding the diamond that Duly Icon had given him and seeking a clue from his grandfather's words. Chris repeated them regularly as he stared at the arches, almost to the point of burning his eyes, even with the protection of sunglasses.

"Find the triangular diamond and bring it to the foot of the bridge! When the two arches meet, you will know what to do."

The supervisor had disappeared without a trace. Chris was at the point of thinking his entire mission had amounted to nothing—no matter what Slash Inaction had said about history and collective memory.

Physically and mentally burned out, Chris tore off his sunglasses and threw them to the ground. He was overheated, thirsty and felt like he was losing his mind.

Instinctively, he shot a final look at the top of the two arches. At the highest point, the three suns lined up, and an exceptionally luminous ray shot through the two arches to land on a metallic panel of the wall behind Chris.

The powerful beam melted the metal, leaving a hole large enough for a hand to pass through.

Chris approached, waved away the smoke and blew on the mark to cool it. The opening was in the shape of a diamond. Wasting no time, Chris pressed his diamond into the spot. The bridge creaked, the earth trembled, and the arches moved as a new ray of light, just as intense as the previous one, took the same path. Chris had just the time to remove his hand. Then he collapsed, eyes closed and motionless.

North Region, Confederate Lands
Gateshead, ex-England – December 25, 2321

Chris' eyelids fluttered. Even with his eyes almost closed, he could glimpse a startling whiteness beyond. He heard faraway music and words he didn't understand.

Dici che il fiume
Trova la via al mare
E come il fiume
Giungerai a me
Oltre i confini
E le terre assetate
Dici che come il fiume
Come il fiume...
L'amore giungerà
L'amore...
E non so più pregare
E nell'amore non so più sperare
E quell'amore non so più aspettare[1]

"Do you like it?" a voice asked. "It's Luciano Pavarotti."

This voice. Chris recognized it immediately.

"It's magnificent, don't you think?" asked Ocarina Jade Mini.

Her long hair caressed Chris' face as she leaned over him.

"Would you like me to translate? It's Italian."

Chris no longer spoke all languages. He had become an ordinary man, and his mission had been accomplished.

"Tell me!" Chris replied. "Tell me what it means,

---

[1] "Miss Sarajevo" from the album "Original Soundtracks 1" by "Passengers"

Ocarina."

She sang:

> *You say that the river*
> *Finds its way to the sea*
> *And as a river*
> *You will come to me*
> *Beyond the borders*
> *And the thirsty lands*
> *You say that as a river*
> *As a river*
> *Love will come*
> *Love...*
> *And I don't know how to pray any more*
> *And in love, I don't know how to hope any more*
> *And for that love, I don't know how to wait any*
> *more...*

Chris opened his eyes. A carpet of sparkling white covered the ground, its chill somehow soothing. He heard the rustling of water from the River Tyne.

"How did you get here?" Chris asked.

"We are back in control, Chris Aftermaths. Men and women are healed, vegetation is thriving, the Confederate Lands are reunited, and technology is once again part of our lives."

Chris lifted his eyes to the arches of the Millennium Bridge, where snowflakes danced. He rummaged around in his pocket. He remembered leaving the old yellowed photo there. The one he'd found in the box from his grandfather.

Chris turned the photo over, and a few snowflakes melted on its back. Blue ink appeared, revealing the following words:

Father Christmas

About the Authors

Aimee Horton, "Survival of the Christmas Spirit"

Aimee is from Lincoln, England, where she enjoys drinking gin and spending time with her family (and she won't tell you which of those she prefers doing). Blogging and overusing social media led her to realize that not only does she love to read but she loves to write... and even more amazingly (to her), people enjoy reading what she writes. Aimee is the author of *The Survival Series* which includes the titles *Survival of the Ginnest*, *Lush in Translation*, *Survival of the Christmas Spirit* and *Mothers Ruined*. For more about Aimee, check out PassTheGin.co.uk.

Vicki Lesage, "All I Want For Christmas Is My Two Front Teeth"

Vicki Lesage proves daily that raising French kids isn't as easy as the hype lets on. In her three minutes of spare time per week, she writes, sips bubbly and prepares for the impending zombie apocalypse. She lives in Paris with her French husband, rambunctious son and charming daughter, all of whom mercifully don't laugh when she says "au revoir." She penned *Confessions of a Paris Party Girl* and #1 Amazon Best Seller *Confessions of a Paris Potty Trainer* in between diaper changes and wine refills, and co-founded indie publishing house Velvet Morning Press. She writes about the ups and downs of life in the City of Light at VickiLesage.com.

Cheryl McAlister, "Noëlle"

Cheryl McAlister is an emerging writer. In addition to "Noëlle," she has three previously published short stories: "Bit By Bit," published by Black Denim Lit, "A Scoop of Henry," in *That's Paris: An Anthology of Life, Love and Sarcasm in the City of Light*, published by Velvet Morning Press, and "The Senescent Logophile," published by The Red Fez. Cheryl has a BFA in painting from the Rhode Island School of Design, and an MFA in Visual Culture from Vermont College of Fine Arts. In addition to her artistic pursuits, Cheryl loves cooking, gardening and animals. Empty nesters, she and her husband, Rick, are embarking on a new stage of their lives focusing on art-making, writing and travel, especially to their beloved France.

Katie Rose Guest Pryal, "Nice Wheels"

Katie enjoys her three professions—novelist, freelance journalist, and lawyer—for one reason: her love of the written word. Fiction or nonfiction, Katie thrives on putting thoughts to paper and sharing them with the world. She lives in Chapel Hill, North Carolina, where the energy of the campus and cafes inspires her writing. Katie is the author of the novel *Entanglement* and the novella *Love and Entropy*. As a freelance journalist, she contributes regularly to *The Huffington Post*, *The Chronicle of Higher Education*, *The Toast*, *Dame Magazine* and other national venues. She's published five books on writing, the most recent with Oxford University Press. You can find her at KatieRoseGuestPryal.com, and you can sign up for her writing newsletter, "Writing Isn't Sexy" (no really, it isn't), at http://bit.ly/pryalnews.

Didier Quémener, "Chris Aftermaths"

Executive chef, private chef, food and wine consultant. Lived in the US, now based in Paris. Does not wear a beret but eats freshly baked bread every day. Cooked his first meal at age seven, graduated from the Sorbonne, worked as a photographer and finally came back to the kitchen where it all started. Didier is French and American, therefore obnoxious, a wine snob and speaks loudly! Didier also contributed to anthologies *Mystery in Mind*, *Legacy* and *That's Paris: Life, Love and Sarcasm in the City of Light*. You can find him at ChefQParis.com and FoodMe.fr.

Laura Schalk, "Joyful Noise"

Laura Schalk is a lifelong bookworm and lover of words. She is American, and has lived and worked in Paris for a decade following stints in Hong Kong, London and New York. Laura works in the corporate sector and pursues her love of creative writing sporadically, during intensive workshops in the summer and in stolen moments throughout the year. Her story "The Little Book of Funerals" was published in the anthology *That's Paris: Life, Love and Sarcasm in the City of Light*.

Acknowledgements

Velvet Morning Press would like to thank our authors for getting into the holiday spirit and writing these stories "off season" so that you may enjoy them during the season!

A big thank you to Ellen Meyer, who made this book look so beautiful that people will want to have it sitting under the Christmas tree.

About Velvet Morning Press

Velvet Morning Press is a boutique publishing house that discovers new authors and launches their careers. VMP publishes fiction in a variety of categories, short story anthologies and special projects involving new and established authors.

Adria J. Cimino and Vicki Lesage are the women behind VMP. Both authors themselves, Vicki and Adria use their experience in writing, editing and marketing to bring the work of other writers to bookshelves. VMP's short story anthologies include *Legacy*, *That's Paris* and *Christmas, Actually*.

If you enjoyed this collection of holiday stories, please consider leaving a review on Amazon—even just a few sentences!

Want more? Get *Recipes & Reads* for free! Simply join Velvet Morning Press's new release mailing list to receive your free copy: http://bit.ly/vmp-news.

A taste of the good life in...
Recipes & Reads

You know that feeling you get after you turn the last page of a great book? It's similar to the feeling you get after enjoying a delicious meal. Satiated. Pleased. Relaxed. Yet… eager for the next slice of goodness!

So, as publishers, readers and food-lovers, we decided to pair our favorite indulgences into this appetizing guide of great reads and great recipes.

Get it for free! Join the Velvet Morning Press new release mailing list and we'll send you a free ecopy of *Recipes & Reads*: http://bit.ly/vmp-news.

And now for a special bonus: "In the Red," a short story from *That's Paris: An Anthology of Life, Love and Sarcasm in the City of Light.*

In the Red

Adria J. Cimino

My parents named me Jing because in Chinese it means calm and quiet. The name would bestow the qualities upon me, according to the fortune teller who advised my mother. But by some weird twist of fate, the naming of me did the opposite. I was emotional, intense and spoke out when Mama told me I shouldn't. And right now, as I ran through the wet street cursing at the bus pulling away from the curb, I was about as far from the definition of my name as anyone could imagine.

But in my situation, it seemed natural to be more than slightly annoyed. I glanced at my watch, fogged up by the rain, and knew I didn't have a choice if I hoped to get to the bank before it closed. I had to run. I tossed my wind-bent umbrella into the trash can and ran like a maniac along the wide boulevard laden with shops and shoppers.

I bumped into several of my countrymen and women who glared at me strangely, surely not expecting to be run over by a frantic, unkempt Chinese girl in the middle of Paris.

It was clear I wasn't one of them any more. I mean

one of the Chinese. When I went home to visit my parents or ran into Chinese tourists in Paris, they heard me speak French, saw me swap chopsticks for a fork. I was no longer quite the same. But I wasn't French either. I had been living in Paris for four years, yet to my dismay, the Parisians still heard my accent, marveled at the symbols I wrote. Sometimes, I felt like a person without a country. I didn't really belong anywhere.

The sight of that familiar, massive glass door broke me from my thoughts and brought me back to the reality of the soggy weather and the problems with my bank account. For an instant, an image stopped me. Gray sweat suit soaked through, a young woman pushed a curtain of wet, black hair back from her pale face. Yet this disheveled picture didn't make me flinch even as I imagined Mama's horrified reaction. Mama wasn't here after all. And I wasn't aiming to impress anyone. I could be as unquiet and untidy as I wanted.

I pushed the door open. My sneakers squeaked on the scratched-up floor. Luckily, a teller was free and no one was ahead of me because I didn't have a second to lose. I tapped my fingers in annoyance on the counter as the woman hid behind her tortoiseshell eyeglasses and a fan of bills. I cleared my throat noisily, but she didn't seem to hear. I promised myself I would wait one more minute, but just as I counted halfway there, she looked up at me.

"May I help you, *Mademoiselle*?" The glasses magnified her light green eyes into water lilies floating in a moon-shaped face. A look of innocence. But it wouldn't shake me.

"My name is Wen. Jing Wen. And there is a big problem with my account. It's in the red and it shouldn't be. I called the bank three times this week. You were supposed to straighten things out but nothing has been done. And then, today, I get this in the mail!"

I tossed the damp, tattered letter onto the counter. It stated that my account not only was in the red, but I owed the bank money because of it. The woman looked it over in slow silence as my heartbeat quickened. Then her fingers rapidly typed something onto her keyboard, and her eyes narrowed as she studied the computer screen.

"The explanation is simple, Ms. Wen. You made too many withdrawals so you were charged withdrawal fees, which drained your account. There's nothing to straighten out."

"But you shouldn't have charged me the fees! That isn't in the contract!"

"It's the way we operate, Ms. Wen…"

My hands shook as I clung to the counter.

"That isn't what Mr. Laurent told me on the phone!" I was screaming now, and my face felt as hot as fire.

"Maybe you didn't understand… Now please lower your voice."

"I understand your language very well! But I will no longer talk with you. Get someone else for me! Now. I have no money because of your mistakes! I can't even buy something to eat tonight."

"Call Pierre," the woman whispered to an alarmed-looking colleague before asking me to wait a moment.

I stomped toward a leather chair to pout and stew over the situation, but I didn't even have the chance to lower myself into the seat. A man who didn't look much older than me approached, presented himself as Mr. Duval and held out his hand. I was about to scowl and push him away, but the expression in his brown eyes soothed me for some strange reason. Still, I wouldn't let my guard down.

I trudged down the hall to his office and repeated the same words I had pronounced only moments earlier. They were as sharp, desperate and angry as the first time.

And my voice was just as loud. Mr. Duval didn't flinch as he listened to me and checked out my account information on his computer.

"Don't worry, Miss Wen," he said. "I'll settle this for you."

"Like the others? You'll say one thing, and then my bank statement will say another."

He shook his head. "We're going to take care of it right now. Some of the newer accounts have withdrawal fees, but yours was opened prior to that. The funds will be back in your account by the close of business tomorrow. In the meantime…"

He reached into a leather bag, extracted a handful of bills and handed them to me.

"What's this for?"

"Your dinner."

When I first came to Paris, I settled in Chinatown. For a day. Mama had friends there and told me I would be comfortable staying with them. It would feel like home. But it wasn't home. Where there should have been lotus flowers, there were roses. Where there should have been silky parasols bobbing in the sunshine, there were only sturdy umbrellas bobbing in the rain. I couldn't pretend this was China or I would be homesick.

So that is how I ended up in the fifth floor walkup about three blocks from the university. The real Paris. The Paris of students, writers, intellectuals. Even if I didn't truly believe it, I still told myself I would become one of them, that I would fit into this city one day. I told myself that eventually, the woman at the bank wouldn't come out with a line like "maybe you didn't understand."

As I gazed now and again at the passersby stopping for bread at the bakery across the street, my hands steadily wrote out the sum I owed Pierre Duval for the previous night's grocery shopping. After all, he had stood by his word. I was in the black.

やくや

I waited for him outside. I didn't want to see any of the others or remember their eyes on me. I figured at closing time, I could catch Pierre Duval alone, as he left. I could have mailed the check, but it seemed like his effort merited a personal thank you. And at least this time, I looked like a human being rather than a drowned rat. As a full-time intern at an investment bank, I had shed my old college attire of jeans and brightly colored T-shirts for pencil skirts and white blouses.

He was laughing, maybe sharing a joke, as he and a colleague exited. His brown hair was disheveled, a reflection of his shirt and tie after hours tucked behind a desk. I took a step forward and was about to call his name, but he had already seen me.

"Is everything OK?"

I nodded and saw relief replace the concern in his eyes. If Pierre Duval knew the Chinese Zodiac, he would say the words my boyfriend Wang said when criticizing my tempestuous behavior: You are too much of a Tiger for your own good. *Or would he?* He was gazing at me with a warm friendliness that washed away any tension of the previous day.

I handed him the check.

"What's this for?"

"For last night's dinner."

He hesitated a moment, glanced down at his toes in a shy sort of way, and then looked up with courage.

"How about if we both use it for tonight's?"

I told myself it was perfectly fine to have dinner with the person who had loaned me money in a moment of need and it didn't represent disloyalty to Wang. (After all, Wang was working in Shanghai and only had sporadic slivers of time for text messages or phone calls. My boyfriend was not dominating my social calendar.)

It didn't matter that Pierre—we were on a first name basis by this point—and I spent two hours talking nonstop over dinner and another two walking along the Seine. I told myself I wasn't the type to swoon because of a bit of male attention and this was about as platonic as platonic could be.

And I told myself the reason I couldn't sleep as I tossed and turned that night was that the stars shining through the skylight were brighter than usual.

❧

Pierre started meeting me after work. The days were getting longer as spring approached summer, and we both enjoyed walking along the Seine and pretending it was still midday rather than early evening. The sun helped us keep up our charade. Pierre was as calm as I was excitable. Together, we were balanced.

He didn't flinch when I told him about Wang. He seemed to accept the limitation of friendship, and I smiled with a sense of relief that I didn't truly feel.

❧

Two weeks passed before the storm known as my mother upset the calm of a warm, sunny afternoon. Barges cruising the Seine cast long shadows upon me as I slouched in my relaxed mode against a willow tree. I didn't see those boats, only felt their presence and heard their sound.

I scolded Mama for interrupting me during the rare break I had from computers, meetings, spreadsheets and four walls. I had exactly 20 minutes. Mama said that gave her plenty of time. She knew I was seeing a young Frenchman. It didn't matter when I told her we were only friends and maybe not even that yet. I could sense her disapproval. Wang was from a good family. The right kind of family. Powerful and respected. I told her my friendships and acquaintances had nothing to do with Wang. I believed my words, but she didn't.

I knew she was shaking her head, pressing her lips together and squinting as I spoke. For my mother, it was clear my rebellious nature would result in a future that wasn't suitable in her eyes. I didn't say anything further. I didn't even bother asking Mama how she found out about Pierre. Mama had a kind of sixth sense, and I didn't question it. She just knew.

৵৽

Pierre called me three times over the next two days, but I wouldn't answer the phone. I told myself my feelings had nothing to do with my mother. I didn't want to admit she still exerted that kind of power in spite of the 5,000 miles separating us. It went against the loud, rebellious side that was the best part of me. I told myself I simply needed more time alone, to focus on my work.

But how long could I really avoid Pierre? My strategy of scheduling out-of-office meetings at the end of each work day couldn't continue forever. I decided to take the initiative and rely on the courage that drove me to the bank many days ago. I called him.

"I'm sorry," I said. "I'm in Paris to succeed, to focus on my internship…" My words seemed wooden, false.

"It's the way I feel that's pushing you away… I couldn't hide it, Jing."

Tears welled up behind my eyes. I was joyful for what I had discovered and sad for what I now was giving away.

"We're different!" I said. "Will I ever fit in here? I don't know… With Wang, the future is clear."

"And that's all you want?" he whispered. "Something easy? What happened to the feisty spirit that brought you to me?"

Don't waver, Jing! an internal voice commanded. I thought of my parents' struggles, their success and their plans for my future. I could no longer lie to myself. This was about my mother and my father. How could I let them down by not following the path they so carefully laid before me? But then another internal voice—the rebellious one—spoke out: *How can you let yourself down?* I ignored it and closed my eyes.

I shut out the beauty of Paris and the memory of our walks along the Seine. I dressed each day in drabness that would help me melt into the crowd. Like a robot, I walked to the bus stop, arrived early at the office, plunged into my assignments and stayed as late as possible. This monotony continued for weeks.

And then, one day, I woke up earlier than usual. It was my birthday. I would have forgotten if it hadn't been for the e-mail from my parents. Not a word from Wang. I didn't know how to feel. I wasn't sure that I really cared.

What to do in Paris at 6 a.m. when sleep won't return? I showered and slipped into a red sundress for good luck in my 24th year. I leaned out the window and watched the early morning action that I always missed: street cleaners flooding the gutters with water, the baker opening his shutters to shed light on golden croissants, a neighbor hurrying his dog to do some business. There was much to see in this city I had been occupying, yet ignoring, over the past several days.

I would forget about the sadness I had created and take a walk along the banks of the Seine.

A knock at the door surprised me as I was gathering up my handbag and change purse.

Pierre. Holding a bouquet of roses in red that mirrored my dress. For luck, love, happiness.

"Don't ever fit in," he whispered.

At that moment, I realized my life and my future were my own.

If you enjoyed this short story, you can check out twenty-seven more Paris-inspired tales in *That's Paris: An Anthology of Life, Love and Sarcasm in the City of Light*!

Additional Titles by Velvet Morning Press

Survival of the Ginnest, by Aimee Horton
Chick Lit/Mom Lit

Meet Dottie Harris. Dottie spent her late 20s working her way up the career ladder, but things are about to change. In this modern-day diary, Dottie, after announcing her pregnancy, turns to social networking to build a new social life. She quickly begins to rely on it—along with gin—as a way to reach out and remind herself of the funny side of the frustrations of motherhood.

Entanglement, by Katie Rose Guest Pryal
Women's Fiction

Awkward 21-year-old Greta Donovan, the fiercely intelligent daughter of a philandering professor, doesn't relate to people nearly as well as she relates to facts and figures. While Greta gets quarks and string theory, she hasn't a clue where men are concerned. She moves to L.A. with her best friend Daphne, a troubled girl with an abusive past. Daphne betrays Greta while throwing a dangerous man in her path. Can Greta survive? Can she forgive?

That's Paris: An Anthology of Life, Love and Sarcasm in the City of Light, featuring a foreword by Stephen Clarke
Multi-Author Short Story Collection

If you've ever traveled to Paris, lived in the City of Light or dreamed of setting foot on its cobblestoned streets, you'll enjoy escaping into this collection of stories about France's famed capital. From culinary treats (and catastrophes) to swoon-worthy romantic encounters (and heartbreaking mishaps), this anthology takes you on a journey through one of the most famous cities in the world.

Legacy: An Anthology
Multi-Author Short Story Collection

What will you leave behind? Long after we've left this world, our legacy remains. Or doesn't. Or remains only in the minds of those who knew us, those whose lives we've touched. Those we've written to, or about. If you had a choice, what mark would you leave? How should people remember you? *Should* they remember you?

Paris, Rue des Martyrs, by Adria J. Cimino
Literary Fiction

Some encounters make a difference. Four strangers in Paris. Each one is on a quest: to uncover a family secret, to grasp a new chance at love, to repair mistakes of the past. Four stories entwine, four quests become one, as their paths cross amid the beauty, squalor, animation and desolation of a street in Paris, the rue des Martyrs.

Close to Destiny, by Adria J. Cimino
Contemporary Fiction/Magical Realism

A story of the role of destiny in life... and of righting the wrongs of the past. Kat, a young woman facing inner demons, is plagued by strange encounters at a London hotel. The experiences make her question her own notion of reality and the power she holds over her own destiny.

Confessions of a Paris Party Girl, by Vicki Lesage
Humor/Memoir

When newly-single party girl Vicki moved to Paris, she was hoping to indulge in wine, stuff her face with croissants, and fall in love. It proved to be much more *difficile* than she'd imagined. In this laugh-out-loud memoir, this cheeky storyteller recounts the ups and downs of her life in the City of Light. Sassy and shamefully honest, Vicki makes you feel as if you're right there in Paris stumbling along the cobblestones with her.

Confessions of a Paris Potty Trainer, by Vicki Lesage
Humor/Memoir

If you think motherhood in America is a challenge, try navigating the City of Light with a stroller in one hand and a croissant in the other. In this riotous memoir, author Vicki Lesage shares the highs and lows of raising her family in Paris.

12956209R00111

Printed in Great Britain
by Amazon.co.uk, Ltd.,
Marston Gate.